PRAISE FOR JOHN VARLEY

"John Varley is the best writer in America."   —Tom Clancy

"My life experience of John Varley's stories has been that the great majority of them are literally unforgettable."
—William Gibson

"There are few writers whose work I love more than John Varley's, purely love."   —Cory Doctorow

"One of science fiction's most important writers."
—*The Washington Post*

"Inventive."   —*The New York Times*

"One of the genre's most accomplished storytellers."
—*Publishers Weekly*

"[Varley] excels in imaginative SF adventure, bringing together an intriguing premise and resourceful characters in a tale of mystery, suspense, and a voyage through time."
—*Library Journal*

"Science fiction doesn't get much better than this."
—Spider Robinson

"Varley is a mind-grabber."   —Roger Zelazny

"Superior science fiction."   —*The Philadelphia Inquirer*

"Varley has earned the mantle of Heinlein."   —*Locus*

BOOKS BY JOHN VARLEY

The Ophiuchi Hotline

The Persistence of Vision

Picnic on Nearside
   (formerly titled *The Barbie Murders*)

Millennium

Blue Champagne

Steel Beach

The Golden Globe

Red Thunder

Mammoth

Red Lightning

Rolling Thunder

Slow Apocalypse

Dark Lightning

Irontown Blues

THE GAEAN TRILOGY

Titan

Wizard

Demon

The John Varley Reader: Thirty Years of Short Fiction

IRONTOWN BLUES

BLUES

John Varley

ACE / NEW YORK

ACE
Published by Berkley
An imprint of Penguin Random House LLC
375 Hudson Street, New York, New York 10014

Copyright © 2018 by John Varley

Library of Congress Cataloging-in-Publication Data

Names: Varley, John, 1947 August 9– author.
Title: Irontown blues / John Varley.
Description: New York : ACE, [2018]
Identifiers: LCCN 2017050549 | ISBN 9781101989371 | ISBN 9781101989388 (ebook)
Subjects: LCSH: Private investigators—Fiction. | Virus diseases—Fiction. | GSAFD:
Science fiction. | Noir fiction.
Classification: LCC PS3572.A724 I76 2018 | DDC 813/.54—dc23
LC record available at https://lccn.loc.gov/2017050549

First Edition: August 2018

Printed in the United States of America
1   3   5   7   9   10   8   6   4   2

Cover illustration by Florian de Gesincourt
Cover design by Judith Lagerman
Book design by Laura K. Corless
Title page art: concrete wall with shadow © Sidorenko Olga / Shutterstock.com

IRONTOWN
BLUES

one _____

The dame blew into my office like a warm breeze off the Pacific. In other circumstances I'd have loved to invite her to do the jitterbug all night long at the Santa Monica Pier to the swinging clarinet of Artie Shaw and the Gramercy Five.

Too bad about the para-leprosy.

She was dressed in retro noir fashion. Her face was a vague outline behind a heavy veil hanging from a hat that had what looked like a peacock on it. Not just the feathers, the whole peacock. Her blouse had frills at the throat, and her jacket had enough shoulder padding that she could have balanced two martini glasses on them. Her shoes had blocky, four-inch heels and open toes, exposing two nails painted carmine. I was willing to bet that her stockings had seams down the back.

Not that I was in any position to scoff at her. She might actually have dressed to fit the setting. My own office could have been transported complete from another era by a time machine.

A rack for hats and coats stood in one corner, with an assortment of hats in various shades of gray. A trench coat hung from one of the hooks. Next to it was a tall metal file cabinet. A ceiling fan above us stirred the air in a desultory fashion. The view out the window was of a pawnshop's neon sign, flashing red and green. In a moment of nostalgic overkill one day I had a paper wall calendar made, and I hung it on the wall. The page showing said April, 1939, the month Raymond Chandler's *The Big Sleep* was published. The artwork above was an illustration of what was known as a pinup girl, dressed in a skimpy bathing suit. Well, skimpy for 1939, anyway.

Most of my office was as phony as the calendar.

The filing cabinet was empty.

The view from the window was a screen animation.

The bloodhound sleeping in the corner was real.

There was no way to tell that we were in a building in a man-made canyon in Luna and that the date was centuries after 1939.

I noticed her gloves. They were gray leather, but there was something wrong with the ends of the fingers. Everything else seemed just the right amount in just the right places.

"Come on in," I said, standing and gesturing to the comfortable oxblood-leather chair in front of my desk. She hesitated a moment longer, then closed the door and walked to the client chair.

"Can I get you a drink? Coffee? Bourbon?"

"No thank you." She turned slightly and gestured to the door. "Am I speaking with Mr. Sherlock or Mr. Bach?"

Printed in gold letters on the pebbled glass in the upper half of the door behind her—backward from here—were the words:

SHERLOCK & BACH
Discreet Private Investigations

"I'm Chris Bach," I said. "Sherlock is my associate, but I only bring him in on certain cases." In the corner behind her, Sherlock lifted his head from the rug and regarded me dubiously, which is the only way he ever regards anyone. He sniffed the air once, didn't seem entirely happy with that, and tried it again. Then he got to his feet, eighty pounds of sad-eyed bloodhound, slouched over to where she sat, and sniffed at her glove.

I was surprised. Sherlock is one of the laziest dogs in Luna and likes to affect a smelled-it-all attitude. A scent that would get him up off his precious rug and across the room for a better sniff must be something very interesting indeed.

The girl was startled to see his huge nose almost touching her left glove, started to jerk it away, then decided against it. Sherlock snuffled up and down the hand, then turned to me and made what I had always interpreted as his version of a shrug. Then he ambled back to his corner and circled around a few times. He lowered his massive head and returned to the serious business of the afternoon nap.

"Now, what can I do for you, Ms. . . ."

"Smith," she said. "Mary Smith."

We professional private detectives train ourselves to keep a poker face.

"I'd like you to find someone for me," she went on. Ninety percent of potential clients want me to follow someone around. Finding someone is usually more interesting.

"What's the party's name?"

"I don't know."

Not necessarily a problem.

"Male or female?"

"The last time I saw him, he was male. But he changes a lot."

A problem Philip Marlowe never had to face. But then I've got resources Phil never had. It evens out.

"Why don't you just start from the beginning?"

"I think I'd better start from the end," she said. She took a deep breath and carefully pulled off one of her kid gloves. It was as if she was so delicate she was afraid not all the fingers would stay in place.

It turned out to be literally true; the ends of all her fingers were missing.

At the last joint on three of them, and the second joint on

the ring finger, was what looked like pink scar tissue. The thumb was intact, but the nail was thickened and twisted, and a painful bluish color. The rest of the hand was covered with an angry red rash.

She let me look at it for a moment, then slipped her glove back on.

"I assume you've heard of lepers?" she said.

"Heard of them, of course. I've even seen one or two."

It's not as if people throw stones and shout "unclean!" as they apparently did in ancient times, back on Old Earth, but lepers are not really welcome in the mainstream of society these days.

Extreme body modifications have been around for a long time, from pierced cheeks to split penises, and that was back in the days when you couldn't unsplit one. These days you can keep a human head alive with no body at all, or elect to have your arms and legs removed for a few weeks, then put back on later. Or not, if that's your twist. It's all socially acceptable. Ain't modern medicine wonderful?

Altering your appearance with engineered diseases has gone through several fashion stages. One decade it's very *in* to sport a suppurating case of psoriasis or tertiary "syphilis," then all of a sudden no one wants to see your faux warts and rashes. Lately it's all pretty *out*. You had to go to some pretty weird dives to see disease heads.

"I have never seen one. It's not my scene at all. But one night I was out enjoying myself . . . enjoying myself rather too much, I guess. I'd had too much to drink. I met a man

5

who seemed nice enough. We talked. One thing led to another, and we ended up in one of the private rooms at the back of the club."

"Which club was this?" I asked, getting out my notebook and pen.

"The Passing Glance," she said. "Level Fifty-six, at the corner of King and Main."

"I know the place."

"I went there when some friends suggested I'd like the floor show. Not an *avant-garde* sort of place at all. In fact, definitely retro." The lady had been slumming, thirty levels from her natural habitat.

"In retrospect, I remember a blister at one corner of his mouth. I discounted it. You know how some people will indulge in a 'beauty mark' here and there.

"The next morning I found my hands were all scaly. Mr. Bach, I'm convinced that he *meant* to infect me." Up to then her voice had been calm and even. Now there was some heat in it. "That he got a *kick* out of it. They call it 'exporting.' The idea is to spread your pet disease to as many straight people as possible."

I thought that I had heard it all, but I admit that was a new one to me. New, and highly illegal. If you are into genetically engineered diseases, they must be *killed* diseases. Noncommunicable. Like old-fashioned vaccines, before humanity really had a good handle on genetics.

I could tell I was going to be looking for a real sicko.

She made a deliberate effort to calm down.

"I think I'd like that bourbon now, if you don't mind," she said.

I got the office bottle from a drawer in my desk. It says Jack Daniel's on the label, but of course it had never been within a quarter million miles of Kentucky. I once had a sip of the real thing, over two hundred years old and costing more than a year's salary from my old job as a bobby, and was disappointed to find that this ersatz stuff tasted just as good. You would think there would be something special about one of the last bottles of booze remaining from Old Earth.

I got two tumblers that looked pretty clean from the drawer. I poured two generous slugs. When the neck of the bottle touched the rim of the first glass, Sherlock's head came up and he huffed once to show his contempt, then got up. He ambled over to the door and stepped on his touch-plate, which opened it for him. He hurried through. Alcohol is not one of Sherlock's favorite scents.

Also, I sometimes drink a bit too much. It's a sad thing when your dog disapproves of you.

"That's quite a . . ."

"Large dog?"

"He's beautiful."

That was never a word I would have applied to Sherlock, but I warmed to her a little for the first time. She was clearly a dog person.

She reached for the glass with both hands, carefully positioned it in the left one, and raised the veil slightly with

7

the right. I caught a glimpse of ravaged features. I had no
desire to see any more.

"What's his name?"

"Watson," I lied. "He's a pedigreed bloodhound. His
nose is very sensitive, and he doesn't like alcohol." I've always wondered how bad the smell of Jack could be to an
animal that thought sniffing another dog's rectum was the
height of pleasure.

"That would sort of spoil his fun, wouldn't it? Warning me?"

We were back to the leper. I was far from convinced it
had all happened the way she said.

"What do you plan to do to him once I've found him? If
you intend to cause him physical harm, I can't help you."

"I'm going to take him to court. But I haven't finished.
Giving me this stuff was bad enough, but normally I'd just
chalk it up to experience. I should have been more careful.
I'm not denying that. So when I started breaking out, I just
went to the medico and told him to cure it."

"But he couldn't cure it."

Her story, apparently, was that it could not be cured.
Which I had a great deal of trouble believing. But for a bad
moment there I felt a little thrill of atavistic fear, fear of
something no one has worried about much for many generations: What if she gives it to *me*?

At some point in human history between the discovery
of fire and the invention of ice cream—humanity's greatest
moment, so far—being eaten by animals stopped being an

everyday thing to worry about. It could still *happen* on Old Earth so long as wild animals remained, but most days you could go about your business—say, in the middle of Manhattan Island—without taking any particular precautions about it.

After the Earth was taken away from humanity by the Invaders, your chances of being preyed upon grew pretty slim since all the feral lions and tigers and bears remained on Old Earth.

It was much later that we were able to stop worrying about disease. It had been several hundred years since anyone got sick from anything other than a self-inflicted condition, i.e., drinking yourself shit-faced and waking up the next day feeling like death. And a damn good thing, too. It would be hard to imagine a better environment for germ-caused disease than the close quarters typical of a Lunar city.

The idea that there might be something incurable out there, something that made your face look like a cross between a beet and a potato, was not a tempting thought.

"So you're telling me this stuff is incurable?"

"Well, no." She suddenly seemed to realize what I was thinking, and held out a hand, palm up. "Oh, no, believe me, if I were still contagious, I'd never have come here. I wouldn't dream of inflicting this on anyone else."

I motioned for her to go on.

"It's just that the *medico* couldn't cure it. He referred me to a gentech lab. They treated me like a fascinating new animal they had discovered. They couldn't cure this thing in one simple step, apparently. Something about its becoming bound up in my genes. They had to make their own custom nanobots to attack it, and they did it in stages. They say I should be back to normal in another week."

I knew her story was not all true, and so what? Clients lie. Every private detective learns that. It's just something you have to work around.

So I opened a desk drawer and got out a standard contract and a pen. She held the pen awkwardly, obviously not having handled one since school, where they still require a minimum of handwriting skills. One day they'll drop the requirement, and we'll finally have achieved that long-predicted goal: the paperless, fully computerized society. And I'll be in big trouble.

When she handed it back, I glanced at the information, written in careful block letters. Under *profession* she had written *artist*. I trust I didn't betray any reaction. Half the nonemployed drones in New Dresden were "artists." What they produced, God alone only knew.

I quoted her my standard rate, a point at which about half my prospective clients hit the road without hiring me. For some reason, many of them expect this sort of work to be cheap. Miss Smith didn't complain. Usually, clients want to thumb payment to me, and they look surprised when I tell them I prefer cash. She had money at hand, in the form of a roll in her purse. She counted out my retainer and laid it on the desk.

"I'll itemize expenses, which you also pay for. If I have to go to Mars or beyond, I'll check with you first."

She nodded. I escorted her to the door and watched her striding down the hallway toward the elevator. So did Sherlock, and after a cautious sniff of the air, he lumbered back into the office before I shut it. He resumed his customary position on the shaggy rug in the corner, first circling it a few times to get his bearings, then plopping down and giving a sigh.

two _____

live in the twenty-mile-long artificial canyon known as the Mozartplatz. It was only about two miles long and a mile wide when it was first opened for business, and from then it kept growing.

Many stories from Old Earth assumed that anyone living on the moon would emulate termites or ants, content to tunnel down into the living rock and conduct their lives without ever seeing much open space. And for the first explorers, hundreds of years ago, that was the case. It was cheap and easy to drill, and the layers of rock over your head protected you from solar storms and cosmic rays.

But—*surprise!*—people didn't like becoming moles. As soon as Lunar society grew rich enough to afford things beyond the daily struggle just to survive—and for quite a while after the Invasion, it was a close-run thing—a natural urge for some space took hold of the habitat builders. Thus the Mozartplatz, and a dozen others like it. But of the densely inhabited planets of the Eight Worlds, only Luna built down instead of up.

It's quite a canyon. Over two miles deep and up to three miles wide in places, each side is shaped into promontories and arroyos reminiscent of Earth's Grand Canyon, if the canyon had been honeycombed with Indian cliff dwellings from top to bottom. At the bottom were lakes and parkland, with here and there a tall building. Trains ran along the trench and crossed on bridges. The sky was filled with various sorts of flying machines, including human-powered ones. Over it all was a quadruple layer of roof, nearly invisible, that turned opaque on a twenty-four-hour day/night schedule during the Lunar day, thus avoiding fourteen-day periods of light and darkness.

When Ms. Smith left, it was getting on toward dusk. I turned off the phony view of a seedy alley in Los Angeles, 1939, and the glass turned transparent. I put my feet up and looked out over the city.

It was dusk, my favorite time of day, when the roof took on an orange tinge. Many lights were coming on. It was a view I never tired of.

My office is on the thirteenth floor of the Acme Building, a faux 1930s high-rise built in what was known as Manhattan Style, trimmed with faux wood and faux bricks. I chose it because I like the era, the time of Chandler and Hammett, Sax Rohmer, Rex Stout, and Mary Roberts

Rinehart. Stone gargoyles line the parapets and spew water when the rain is turned on. There is a turning searchlight atop the huge radio mast on the roof. The word "ACME" in red neon flashes from all four sides.

I stayed at my window until it was almost dark, nursing a glass of bourbon. My chair creaked as I got up, and Sherlock was instantly awake, looking at me with the intensity only a dog who is about to play can muster. I let him suffer for a moment, then headed for the door.

"Ready to go home, boy?"

He was already in motion, plunging through the door flap and clattering down the corridor and hitting the touchplate that opened the stairway door. He was through it and on his way down before I reached the elevator.

It's a game we play. Actually, is it a game if he always wins? Because he does, you know. My dog always finds his way home faster than I do. I don't know how he does it. I suppose I could find out if I fitted him with a tracker, but my feeling is that even a detective should have some mystery in his life. Besides, it would be cheating.

Down at the ground floor of the Acme Building, I unchained my bicycle and swung aboard. The office is about a mile from the south end of the 'Platz, and my home biome is nearly at the north end, a journey of at least eighteen miles, but actually longer because of the serpentine route I was forced to take, avoiding lakes and other obstacles. Cycling almost forty miles a day is a bit too much for me, but simply boarding the monorail at the Acme stop was far too little. By biking a few miles along the path and getting off a mile short of my stop, I not only got daily exercise but avoided gym fees. It suited me fine.

I boarded the train, folded up my bicycle, and found a seat. This time of day there usually was one, another good reason to linger at the office and let the rush-hour crowd thin out. Mozartplatz keeps a more or less nine-to-five workday, and varies the hours of sunlight or artificial light when Luna's farside turns its back on the sun so that we have "seasons," though we don't go so far as to make it too cold or too hot, except in isolated disneylands.

Darkness had fallen by the time I got off the rail at my stop. I biked to the down escalator and hopped aboard. It's about a quarter of a mile ride to the 51 level, where I got off. I passed through a safety air lock, which I had only seen closed during monthly blowout drills, and into a nondescript tunnel with air locks every few hundred meters on each side leading to some of the thousands of Earth habitat re-creations that riddle the sides of Mozartplatz. At the third one on the right I slapped the palm reader and walked into another world, one that had never actually existed.

Home, for me, is Noirtown, a medium-sized habitat popular with twentieth-century American reenactors. It is one long street, zigzagging here and there so you can't see from one end to the other, themed to dates circa 1910 to around 1960. You enter at 1910, to find "automobiles" from that era parked at the curbs. None of them actually run, of course. Except for surface transportation, no one has owned an autonomous private vehicle since the Invasion. Turn the corner and you're in 1920, then one more corner to the street where I live, in the 1930s.

The architecture is a mix of New York, Chicago, and Los Angeles buildings. I live in a two-bedroom flat on the second floor of a Hollywood Boulevard building above an Italian restaurant, the Monte Carlo. Outside my front window is a large neon sign that flashes on and off all night, in green, red, and blue. Which means that it flashes all the time, because in Noirtown, the sun never comes up. If I raise a window and lean out a little, I can see all the way through the 1940s, into the 1950s, where an oversized "moon" hovers over the jagged pagoda of the Chinese Theater. The moon never moves.

The theater is phony, just a façade with a marquee that changes daily. Right now it claimed to be showing *Ben-Hur*, "Winner of 11 Academy Awards," starring Charlton Heston and Stephen Boyd.

The restaurant is real. I eat a lot of my meals there. If you visit, try the minestrone. It's the best in Luna.

It rains a lot in Noirtown, which adds to the atmosphere. It was raining now as I made my way up the gloomy, worn wooden stairs to my apartment door.

Sherlock was sprawled on his rug in the front room, pretending to be asleep but breathing too hard to be convincing.

"How do you do it, old sport?" I asked, as I flung my gray fedora at the hat rack, missing the hook as usual. He lifted his head briefly, said *Where the hell have you been?*, chuffed noisily, and lay down again. I knew the answer had something to do with the hidden service passages that most of us seldom see, and that he was helped out by the little chip in his head and the locator app that contained a detailed map of the whole 'Platz . . . and it didn't hurt that he was genetically augmented to be a lot smarter than any dog that ever sat around a caveman's fire and waited for scraps to be thrown his way. Still, it just didn't seem possible that he could be that fast.

I once entertained the paranoid notion that he was actually two dogs, identical twins who hung around the apartment and the office just to fool me.

Since it is always night in Noirtown and I won't allow a timepiece eye implant   or any other sort of cyber enhancements—I always wear a watch. I consulted it now. Mickey's little hand was pointing to the eight, and his big hand was just about to the one. Too late to really get moving on the Mary Smith case, but far too early for bed.

I went to the Frigidaire and got a simulated beef bone. I tossed it to Sherlock, who lifted his head once again and regarded it with contempt, then got back to some serious sleeping.

Time for dinner.

I hurried down the street to 1940, Chicago, and an establishment called the Nighthawk Diner. It's a big L-shaped lunch counter that serves a decent cup of coffee and okay brontoburgers, though they don't call them that on the menu. Just about all the patrons order the blue plate special, which is whatever Whitey, the proprietor, decides it will be that day.

About half the stools were filled with the usual assortment of residents and outsiders there to sample the atmosphere of the habitat. I made my way toward the end of the counter, where there are some booths, and the lighting is dim and spotty. On the way, I signaled to Whitey for the special and a beer. He nodded. Whitey is a man of few words.

I had come to the Nighthawk hoping to find one of my best informants, a man I knew only as Hopper. The Hopster doesn't exactly deal in anything illegal, but he knows most of the people in the 'Platz who do. He deals in information and seems to make a pretty good living at it. His clothes are always the best quality, favoring exotic embroidered silks from some Chinese dynasty. He tops it off with a Fu Manchu mustache. But he doesn't look the least bit Chinese. He looks like a weasel crossed with a crocodile. His information is always good, though.

I slid into the booth opposite him.

"What do you know about leprosy?" I asked.

"Always straight to the point, eh, gumshoe?" He smiled, showing two rows of pointed teeth. He always talks to me in hard-boiled dialect he picked up from reading old detective novels he read just so he could irritate me.

"Ixnay on the abgay," I said. "Why should I spend a lot of my time on a two-bit grifter? You're already into my pocket for a lot of dough."

"All reet, Jackson." He paused and looked thoughtfully at the tin shade of the hanging light fixture as Flo, the waitress, set a long-necked bottle and a glass in front of me. The cap was still on the bottle. I picked up the church key—don't you just love some of those twentieth-century slang terms?—and popped the top off. Hopper watched as I carefully poured the cold golden liquid down the side of the glass. It came out with just the amount of head I like on my brew.

"Leprosy, leprosy," Hooper said, tugging on one side of his soup strainer and pretending he was trying to recall where he had heard the term. "Seems I've heard it's going out of style with the sick set. It was big a few years ago. Now all the hip daddies and dollies are getting back to basics. Things like lupus, psoriasis, hives, even plain old acne. What used to be 'entry-level' bugs. Of course, there are always the hard-core sickies, the ones who go for the really dramatic disfigurements. Necrotizing fasciitis, erysipelas, seborrheic keratosis, really nasty stuff."

Hopper was eyeing me skeptically. "So what's your interest?" he asked. "I never thought that was your scene."

"That's none of your concern," I said. "What I want to know isn't who is taking it, or wearing it, or whatever these people call it. I'm trying to find people who are spreading it."

He drew in a quick breath. I think I had succeeded in shocking him for the first time in our relationship.

"You mean involuntary infection?"

"That's exactly what I mean. Also, the bacterium seems to have been engineered to be damn near incurable."

His frown grew even deeper.

"You're talking some serious shit here, my friend."

"Be that as it may, I need to find out where to go to contact these people."

"I guess you know that the penalty for that is around a century in the icehouse on Sedna. Which means the nuts who do it are both crazy and ruthless. They would kill you without a second thought."

"Still, I need to know."

He said nothing. For some reason he seemed reluctant to give me the straight dope on this thing. But I could wait him out. To hurry him up, I laid some filthy lucre on the table.

"I only heard of these folks recently," he said. "I thought I had heard it all, but this one shocked me." He scrawled something on the napkin. He held on to it for a moment. I pushed the wampum toward him. He shook his head and slid out of the booth.

"This one's on the house," he said. I expect my eyebrows climbed almost to my hairline. This was not Hopper's style.

I looked at the napkin and felt a chill run up my spine.

It was an address in Irontown.

"Irontown," I muttered.

Flo slapped the blue plate special down on the table in front of me and gave me a funny look. The food looked like some kind of goulash. I pushed it away from me. Suddenly I wasn't hungry.

three _____

You would think that, this far into the Information Age, somebody would know when Irontown became known as Irontown, and why. And you would be wrong. I did a major search and found nothing but rumors and folktales and rock-rat legends.

It obviously isn't really made out of iron. Irontown is made of steel, plastics, ceramics, and nanotubes, just like everywhere else.

Everybody knows where Irontown is, of course. Ask anyone; they can point you to it.

Except they can't. Not really.

Its boundaries are vague. It's not like you are walking down a decrepit, badly lit corridor, with the sound of water dripping somewhere in the distance and the smell of something rotting and the occasional screech of a feral bat—though you will usually encounter those things and more on your way there—and suddenly you find yourself in Irontown. There are no signs saying WELCOME TO IRONTOWN!, no Chamber of Commerce placards announcing the presence of the Freemasons, Shriners, Tongs, Elks, and Yakuza, or inviting you to attend services at the Church of Elvis or Jay-Dubyas or Hubbardites.

What happens is the passage gradually grows gloomier, the lights more flickery, the smells more pungent, the people more furtive, until you begin to encounter some people you definitely wouldn't want to take home to meet Mama.

To understand Irontown you have to go back to the very beginning, in the days just after the Invasion.

There were only five Lunar colonies when the Invaders showed up from interstellar space and forcibly and fatally evicted humanity from Earth. The total population was around seven thousand. Luna in those days has been compared to Antarctica in the early twentieth century, both in terms of population and the harshness of the environment. But at least at McMurdo Station you didn't have to import or make your own oxygen.

Beyond Luna there were three bases on Mars, with less than a thousand inhabitants, and isolated research stations in the Outer Planets. They vanished as completely as did about eight billion humans on Earth.

One of the Martian beachheads quickly suffered a catastrophic failure. The same happened to one of the Lunar bases. So the total number of survivors of the Great Death was around five thousand. Those five thousand Founders contained the entire available gene pool of humanity.

The first decades were very, very tough.

It was touch and go, the people surviving from day to day. Everyone was required to work, and work very hard. Water had to be located and mined, in Luna and on Mars. Power plants had to be maintained. Food had to be grown. Sixteen-hour workdays were the norm, and twenty-hour shifts not uncommon. Some died of malnutrition or sheer exhaustion.

But they made it, those hardy survivors. It is no wonder that schoolchildren to this day sing of the pioneers, and that every year we commemorate the Invasion with defiant promises: *Next year on the Earth!*

It's a pretty hollow promise by now.

———————

As more and more babies arrived, more habitat had to be carved out for them, naturally. The earliest Lunar dwellings were rude, cramped, and hazardous. People began to move underground. Mazes of tunnels and rooms connected in a haphazard way, with little planning at first.

With the passing of another century, life had become easier than it had ever been, even on Old Earth. The population exploded, and more space was needed to accommodate them.

People demanded, and got, many more options in life. They no longer wished to live in tunnels and caves, no matter how luxurious. They wanted open spaces, as much as that was possible on an airless moon. And it turned out to be quite possible. The first disneys were built, ten miles across, twenty miles, fifty miles. Each contained a different ecology, patterned after the lands of Old Earth. Animals and plants were created from the vast DNA banks that had survived the years of crisis. The land inside the disneys was sculpted and furnished. When inside one, the illusion was complete. Except for the low gravity, you might imagine you were in Kansas or Congo, the Swiss Alps, the Sahara, a Pacific island, or the Russian tundra.

While this was going on, the vast canyons like the Mozartplatz were being dug. For those who were not interested in the sweeping vistas offered by the various 'Platzes, there was another option for living illusions: simulated neighborhoods like the one I live in.

Lunarians now live in a society so rich, so luxurious, offering so many options to just about everyone, that those few thousand Founders would scarcely have been able to imagine it. Energy is cheap and almost unlimited. Labor is mostly done by machines more deft and powerful than human hands. Standardization is a thing of the past. You can design your own clothes or furniture or bathroom or objet d'art and have it printed and delivered within the hour.

Tired of living in an environment that simulates a medieval castle courtyard? Prefer to live on a St. Louis street from the year 1900, but one doesn't exist? Just put your desire up on a board and if you can find a few dozen, maybe a hundred others of the same mind, a developer will be happy to dig out enough space and fill it with clapboard houses with front-porch swings, big oak trees in the yard, and a dog named Spot.

————

Though there is no sign approaching Irontown warning you as you enter that "From here on in, you're on your own," there really ought to be. Or maybe "Here be dragons!" Or "Your remains will not be sent back to your relatives."

Remember those ancient habitats, the no-frills corridors and caverns that the first, second, and third generations of Lunar survivors lived in? They are still there. No one ever bothered to fill them in, or wall them off. They are almost all abandoned, owned by no one, and yet still a part of the city. They have air and water and are kept at temperatures compatible with human life. But who would want to live there?

One answer is simple: losers.

Somewhere beneath every apparent paradise like the Mozartplatz, there exists a subculture of people who have opted out.

Some people are born criminals, sociopaths, violent offenders. They are just unable to learn to get along with others. They usually end up with long prison sentences. Many opt to go to Irontown when they get out, if they don't force the police to kill them first.

Then there are the "tinfoil-hat" people: paranoids, delusional, what my mother used to call barking mad or fucking nuts. Many of them wind up in Irontown, where no one cares if they stand on a street corner and preach about the Galactic Emperor Xenu or warn of the end of the universe.

There are hoarders, people who fill their apartments with junk they can't part with. They can hoard freely in Irontown.

There are some people who think of themselves as political refugees. The government is out to imprison them, and they feel safer from the forces of tyranny when in their little Irontown enclaves. Those at the extremes of libertarianism and capitalism and communism, anarchists, weird religious cults. Heinleiners.

There is a certain percentage of people who really dare not leave Irontown because they are wanted for a crime. The great advantage to them is that the police seldom visit Irontown, and only in groups of four or more, and only in search of the most extreme criminals.

Other than that, law enforcement leaves Irontown alone. The authorities turn a blind eye to the place, viewing it as an important safety valve for the world's malcontents. Good luck getting a cop or a bobby to investigate a crime committed in Irontown.

Why, you may ask, as many people do, have we not stamped out crime and criminals, misfits, the disturbed and the insane?

The scary fact is, we could. Mind-altering techniques exist to turn the most obstreperous sociopath into a mild-mannered, productive, genial—though rather dull—model citizen. And, of course, if someone persists in psychotic behavior that threatens the peaceful members of the populace, they can be confined.

But a cornerstone of the civilization we fought so hard to establish after the Invasion is the sanctity of the mind. Unless someone asks for help, actually *wants* to have a spoon stuck into his or her cerebrum and have it stirred into a more average consistency, society is forbidden to interfere.

You have the inalienable right to do any fool thing you want to do as long as it doesn't endanger others.

My going to Irontown was certainly a damn fool thing to do.

After dinner I nursed a bourbon and looked out at Noirtown.

Sherlock was curled up in his bed. But he couldn't seem to get comfortable. He looked up again, took a few deep sniffs, then lumbered to his feet and ambled over to where I sat, bathed in the alternating neon glows of red, blue, and green. He used his muzzle to slip his head under my hand, and I found myself scratching him behind his big, floppy ears. He looked up at me again, mournfully.

There was no way to fool Sherlock's sense of smell. He had detected the distinct odor of fear from across the room.

four _____

Any of my pulp-fiction heroes would have gone charging toward Irontown, trench-coat collar up against the drizzling rain, fedora riding casually on his head, his gat loaded with six lead pills and firmly jammed into the leather shoulder holster. However . . .

Ms. "Smith's" disease was not going to kill her nor infect anyone else. There was no ticking time bomb. I could take my time, and ever since the Big Glitch, I always take time to study the situation before rushing headlong into danger.

No, I needed time to think, to come up with an approach. And when I need to think, there is one thing I do that usually helps with that. I moonlight as a bobby.

————————

Our police force is layered, its functions divided.

None of the Eight Worlds has what you could call a standing army, though a few have small navies; in fact, since the

Invasion no one has much of a military at all. Who would we fight? A space war might attract the attention of the Invaders, and nobody wants that. The last time they noticed us we nearly became extinct.

So though there are endless trade disputes and other reasons for any and all of the major planets to get angry about, war in space is impractical, no matter what the writers of thrillers might tell you. No one has even talked seriously about going to war with anyone in my lifetime, and for at least a century before.

Luna and some of the other planets have a voluntary paramilitary, strictly monitored and severely limited in scope, because rebellions, insurrections, uprisings, and even full-fledged revolutions have happened. There was a bad one on Oberon only ten years ago. Mars has had three violent upheavals since the Invasion. Luna had one about fifty years after the Invasion.

At the patrol level, police work largely consists of keeping order in the streets and rounding up felonious perpetrators . . . to use a bit of cop-speak. More commonly known around the precinct as the more technical term, dirtbags.

Then we get down to the level of misdemeanors, and we have a separate force for that, popularly known as bobbies. The equivalent back on Old Earth might have been traffic cops. We bobbies walk the corridors and the wide-open spaces, issuing summonses to litterbugs, jaywalkers, staggering drunks, and other menaces to society.

Okay, it's not glamorous, but as the guy said whose job was to sweep up after the dinosaurs in the circus, at least I'm still in show business. So I'm still in police work.

I find it oddly relaxing to be out on patrol. As for Sherlock, it's what he lives for. He loves it best when he tracks down the violator himself. After all, he is a bloodhound.

———

Sherlock is too obedient and far too smart to ever need something as gross as a leash, real or electronic. But the closest he comes to that indignity is when he is on the trail, or on the hunt. He lopes ahead of me, snuffling along the ground or hoovering great drafts of air into his mighty snoot, which is said to be one million times more sensitive than the human snoot and about four or five times more sensitive than any other dog breed.

The man I got him from as a puppy claimed the best bloodhounds "could track a mouse fart across a square mile of shit" and I've never had any reason to doubt that assessment. It is sheer pleasure to watch him cast about from right to left, left to right, to figure out which direction a fleeing desperado has run by the intensity of the scent he left behind.

He's impossible to fool, and he never falls for any of the old traps, like spreading ground pepper or dried cat urine behind you. He detects that a mile away, from the tiniest trace, and just goes around it. Once in a great while a repeat offender gets an unexpected visit from me to explain the consequences of trying to hurt my dog. The explanation seldom results in broken bones but is apt to entail a little bruising. It never results in any charges against me. Sherlock is adored by all the regular cops in the neighborhood.

———

Today we were in hunt mode, not tracking, so his nose was held high, sampling the breezes. We weren't looking for any particular person, we were seeking *anybody* who wasn't in compliance. That can mean several things, but most of the time it is OAPH, Offences Against the Public Hygiene. Sherlock and I intended to catch a few reckers.

There can be a broad range of disagreement on what is a great smell, a good one, a neutral one, a bad one, a terrible one. But there are some that are almost universally loathed, never to be allowed out in public.

The list of these is surprisingly long, and every year it grows by a few as petitions are submitted and put to a vote concerning one scent or another. Right now Sherlock is authorized to seek out and report to me when he detects one of five hundred and seventeen distinct smells.

We live close together in a closed environment. There are dozens of layers of air scrubbing, of course, but no system like that is perfect. We simply can't allow someone to pollute the environment that millions of people have to live and work in.

And wouldn't you know it, if anything is forbidden, there are some people who will crave it intensely.

Many people were incensed (so to speak) at the narrow options for permissible odors, such as burning incense. Years ago they would hold "burn-ins," and invite arrest, but it didn't do them any good. They can still burn the nasty stuff at home, or as part of religious ceremonies in air-isolated and filtered churches.

Scenting oneself in various ways is quite an ancient custom. People have devoted their lives to the identification and concoction of exotic essences, but as more and more people were won over to the side of smeller's rights, they saw one formulation after another put on the proscribed list. It eventually reached the point where only the blandest, most nearly undetectable perfumes were permitted.

The situation that prevails now seems to satisfy most people. You can wear scent at home, and there are clubs and bars and dance floors and such where you can drench yourself in Chanel #5.1 to your heart's content, just as long as you shower thoroughly before you leave.

Another thing that should have surprised no one is that anything that is forbidden will acquire a cachet among some people, become a trendy thing, a hip thing, something that "everybody is doing." The darkest side of the scent fetish involves something that you would think would appeal only to dogs, who seem to find the smell of other dogs' butts to be endlessly fascinating, and probably quite wonderful. I've asked Sherlock about it, but as usual, he is silent on the matter.

But in police work you encounter pretty much any type of human behavior there is, and we are all aware of an underground that enjoys really nasty smells. It stays underground because most people don't really want their neighbors to know that they host stench parties. Most citizens would be repulsed by the idea of people sitting around inhaling the smells of stale sweatsocks, vaginal yeast infections, and rotten fish.

When Sherlock picks up a scent, he comes as close as he ever does to losing control. He does everything but grab me by the trouser leg and pull me where he wants to go.

He never howls during the chase, but makes a high-pitched and almost inaudible whine. *The game is afoot, Bach,* he seems to say. *Why are you lagging behind?*

Now he raised his nose as high as it would go and tensed all over. In other breeds the ears would have stood up straight, but the best Sherlock can do with his enormous earflaps is shake them sharply, making a sound like a wet towel snapping.

Then he was off to the races.

Even though I was jogging, he quickly left me in the dust.

His limit is about fifty meters ahead of me. When he reaches that point, the GPS chip in his head gives him an alert, and he stops. If he is still casting around, he will come back to me, but if he is on the trail, he will just stop and wait for me to catch up, fidgeting impatiently. He never faces away from the scent. When I catch up, he resumes the track.

We only nailed one desperado. I was feeling vaguely depressed when we returned to the apartment. The whole purpose of wasting a day harassing the olfactory challenged was to come up with an approach to entering Irontown without endangering my one and only hide. I had come up blank.

I figured it was time to go to Mom for help.

five _____

SHERLOCK'S TAIL

TRANSLATOR'S NOTE

Since the art and/or science of interpretive assisted translation of
the thoughts and experiences of Cybernetically Enhanced Canines
(CECs) is new and still developing, it seems useful to introduce this
account with a short explanation of what it is, and what it is not.
Most people have never had contact with a CEC and may have only
a vague idea of what one is, and even less of an understanding of
how interpretive assisted translation works. Therefore, this prefa-
tory tutorial will begin with the basics.

First, the method.

Genetically modified companion animals have been around for

a century. They were built on the foundations of knowledge gained by the creation of genetically modified food plants and animals, which have been around much longer. Most animal GMCAs were created with the instinct for aggression and predation turned off, backed up, of course, with implants that render the animal unconscious if violent behavior threatens. It was not possible in the past to have a full-grown tiger or bear as a suitable companion for a child. That news comes as a shock to many pet owners. This writer invites the reader to look at old nature documentaries to learn how dangerous these big, lovable, affectionate creatures could be.

Unlike other animals, dog GMCAs were engineered with transplanted and custom-made genes mainly intended to enhance their intelligence, since violent canine behavior toward humans a dog regards as "pack" was largely bred out of the species thousands of years ago. The only additional work needed was to extend this "created instinct" of nonaggression to all humans. Today, all dogs (except those trained for security work and guard duty) have this happy trait.

The next step in the first real in-depth communication between human and animal was the implantation of neural nets, very similar to those in most humans, in enhanced dogs. If done during puppyhood, it has been shown that a dog is capable of interfacing with the neural-net cloud, just as humans can. This is not possible with "normal" dogs.

What a translator/interpreter does is tune in on the thoughts passing between the cloud and the dog, and between the translator and the dog, and between the cloud and the translator. This three-way hookup enables the translator to understand what the dog is "saying."

Misconception: The intelligence of an enhanced dog is about equal to an IQ of 70 in a human being. This is true, but an unfair comparison. Rather than a mentally challenged human, the dog should be compared to other dogs, in which case it is best regarded as a genius.

A problem with an untrained person attempting interfacing with a CEC dog is that dogs do not think in "words." That is, they do not string together concepts such as "food" and "eat" to make sentences: "I want to eat food." Nevertheless, they do have thoughts that can be expressed in words, though a translation of such must always be accompanied by a disclaimer that the interpretation is probably not 100 percent accurate. The best translators have been shown to be 97 percent right, to the extent such matters can be tested. Each certified CEC translator is tested by the Translator Examining Board (TEB) of the Cybernetically Enhanced Canine Translators Association (CECTA) and assigned a ranking, from novice to adept. (This adept translator has a confirmed score of 96 percent, but believes the examiners misunderstood part of one answer!)

Dogs do understand what we call "pronouns," knowing the difference between self and other, between me, you, and they. Their translated statements can be accepted, subject to limitations, as witness testimony in misdemeanor proceedings.

Misconception: Dogs do not remember events for very long. Again, this is true of normal dogs. It has been shown that a puppy *does not remember having made a mess for much more than a few minutes, and so is mystified as to why she is being scolded. Adult dogs are not much better. Most animals, except higher primates, are not time-binding in the sense of remembering things sequentially.*

Learning in most animals is a process of imprinting by repetition. Thus, an ordinary dog can be taught many different tasks, but will not understand them the way humans do. Repetition of a command such as "sit," emphasized by a reward of food or affection, will build a pathway in a dog's brain. When he hears the word "sit!" he will sit, without really knowing why he is doing it except that he feels better for having done it.

This is not true of CECs. Their memories for events is as good as our own, partly because of the enhancement of their brains and partly because of the neural net that enables them to store information in the cloud, just as we do. This relates to events and their sequences only, what we call the passage of time. Did something happen five minutes ago, five days ago, or five years ago? CECs can tell you.

All dogs are just as good at storing memories of the things they see as we are, and much, much better at remembering sounds and, especially, scents.

Interpretation of scents, in fact, is the major stumbling block in a translator's job. There are simply no words, no concepts, in any human language, for the incredible wealth of sensory data in the huge part of a dog's brain that deals with smells. One translator/ interpreter has likened the tiny bit of such "scentsory" data we can experience from interfacing with a dog to a human shut up in a black box and able to perceive the universe only through the tiniest hole. We are awed by what little we can see and are tantalizingly aware that we are seeing only a thousandth of what is out there! There seems to be no way around this barrier. It would be like teaching a blind cave fish to see.

Misconception: Dogs have no sense of humor. Once more, it is true that normal dogs do not. CECs, however, have a well-developed sense of humor. Their notion of a good laugh tends to be quite basic, and often bawdy. They love a good pratfall, a pie in the face, or frightening a cat. Most people do not realize this, because even CEC dogs do not laugh. They are not physically equipped for it, just as their faces are not equipped to show many emotions. (They use their tails or their whole bodies to express their feelings.) But they are laughing inside.

One more word about CEC humor. To the astonishment of everyone involved in their creation and in interfacing with their minds, it is indisputable that some of the very smartest CECs appreciate puns. They do not experience them quite as we do. They enjoy the tension between two words that sound the same (homophones) but can have two different meanings. When a human barks "hair," meaning threadlike strands growing from the skin, and "hare," meaning a rabbit, CECs find this deliciously funny. They cannot distinguish between the spellings, of course, because they cannot read. (So far, but tune in tomorrow!)

That should do as an introduction to the account you are about to examine. And though I was urged to make all my remarks in the third person, I am finding this far too stilted and impersonal, so *from now on I will appear in the first person. From time to time in this account I will insert parenthetical remarks when I feel clarification is needed.*

> —Penelope Cornflower
> Certified CEC Adept (TEB 96%) Translator
> Sector 54, 1700 Leystrasse, Suite 120
> King City, Luna

Hello, my name is Sherlock. Bark! Arf-arf! Bow-wow! Ha-ha-ha! That is a dog joke. I do not really bark any of those things. I do not know why humans say dogs do bark those things. Humans can be very stupid.

(A note already: This is what I meant by dog humor. The joke is probably best understood by another dog. You will discover as you go along that Sherlock does not have a very high opinion of humans.—PC)

I am Sherlock, and this is my tail. I am telling it or wagging it. You figure it out. Humans can be very stupid.

(See what I mean about puns! And I will omit Sherlock's opinion of humans most of the time, as he follows most of his statements with that thought.—PC)

Hello, my name is Sherlock. I will now tell you some things about myself.

I am five years old. I remember things very well, but I do not remember being born, and I do not remember when I was very young. The first thing I remember is when AlphaChris picked me up at the kennel for the first time. AlphaChris smelled good. I remember licking his face. I remember him smiling and scratching my ears. I liked being picked up. I like having my ears scratched. I do not like being picked up anymore.

(Sherlock knows the man's name, but his thoughts about him are more complex than just a name. People with dogs are usually called owners or masters. Neither word seems appropriate in the case of the relationship between Christopher Bach and Sherlock. It might be more accurate to say they are partners, but the word that best describes Sherlock's place might be "sidekick," in the sense of fictional stories. In such stories there is always a subservient or second-fiddle figure, a Sancho Panza to the protagonist, Don Quixote. So, ironically, Sherlock best fills the role of Dr. Watson in the Arthur Conan Doyle stories.

(It must be emphasized that the important thing, in Sherlock's eyes, is that he accepts Chris as alpha in his pack. The pack is small, consisting of just the two of them, but that is of no consequence to Sherlock. The alpha male of the pack makes the decisions and gives the orders.——PC)

I am five. I have trouble with numbers. I can count to ten but I lose track after that. I have my own number system, though. It goes one, two, three, four, five, six, seven, eight, nine, ten, many. After that there is a lot, a whole lot, one hell of a lot, and a shitload.

I am five. I have learned that a big dog like myself might live as long as fifteen years. That is a ten and a five. I have learned that fifteen is not as long as humans live. I have

learned that everything dies. I do not completely understand what it is to not-be, but I have seen dead things. They
do not move and they are cold and they smell of death.

Living fifteen years does not seem fair to me. I am beta
male. When I am gone, αChris will have no one in his pack.
I think this will make him sad. But αChris says life is not
fair. He is alpha, so he is probably right. αChris also says
that maybe I can go to the vet and get treated so I live longer. Humans live a lot longer. Maybe a shitload longer. I
would like that. I do not want to not-be.

I am the breed known as bloodhound. I have learned
that all dogs are ninety-nine percent wolf. Ninety-nine is a
large number. I have seen wolves in the zoo. They are not
smart like me. I am very smart. But they smell like dogs.

My coat is brown and short and very beautiful. My ears
are loose and hang down and they are beautiful, too. People want to touch them because they are pleasant to touch.
I do not mind being touched on the ears. I have a big beautiful nose. I do not like my nose to be touched. I have big
beautiful jowls, but I do not slobber like some dogs do.
Much.

*(Dogs have no modesty, and do not lack self-confidence. CECs
are especially aware of their talents.——PC)*

I cannot read. I have tried to read but the little black
spots of different shapes begin to move like bugs and crawl
around the page. I would like to read. Maybe they will fix
me someday so I can read. αChris likes to read old books.

They are made of old paper and old ink and old glue. I like the way they smell. For now I enjoy looking over αChris's shoulder as he reads. Then I fall asleep.

(The issue of what to call Mr. Bach in this account is one I debated internally for some time. In a formal story he would be "Bach," just as one of his pulp-fiction heroes was always known as "Marlowe." But Sherlock is anything but formal.

(Then there was Christopher, or just Chris, and I almost went with the latter. But it did not convey the flavor of what was going on in Sherlock's mind when he thought of his partner.

(Finally there was the standard way of looking at a human-canine relationship, which would be to call him "Master," or "Master Chris." That one stuck in my craw even worse because although it was true in a way—Chris was certainly the boss in their relationship—Sherlock felt himself entitled to more leeway in that regard than a normal canine.

(In the end I went with the Greek prefix, α, and Chris: αChris. Every time Sherlock thinks about Mr. Bach, his status as alpha dog in the pack is uppermost in his mind. One's standing in the pack is paramount, it trumps everything. Sex, in comparison, is relatively unimportant . . . except at certain times of the year, of course. He never thinks simply "Chris." His rank is always in the forefront. So I have chosen to present Bach in that manner every time Sherlock thinks of him in this story.—PC)

I like watching movies. I do not always understand what is going on, but I like to watch, anyway. I wish they had a scent. That would make them much better. αChris prefers movies from long ago. These movies are usually about humans trying to find something. Detective stories. We are detectives, me and αChris. I like finding things. Sometimes the movies have dogs in them. I have seen *Lassie Come Home* many times. I always worry that Lassie will not find her way back to Joe, who is portrayed by Mr. Roddy McDowell, but she always does. I would like to sniff Mr. Roddy McDowell, but αChris says he has passed on. That makes me sad. I would like to sniff Lassie's ass. What a beautiful bitch!

(Sherlock obviously does not know that Lassie was a male dog. I have been careful not to let him learn that.

(By now you may have noticed that Sherlock shares a trait with most other CECs, and that is difficulty sticking to the subject at hand. He is apt to go haring off along side trails and only get back to his story when he feels like it. I have made decisions as to what to include and what to omit. I will leave in most of his observations regarding odors, since they are so important to Sherlock. At other times some judicious editing seems the best idea. Here, for instance, he tells in great detail of the movie dogs he likes. He covers all eras, from Grayfriars Bobby and Rin-Tin-Tin, through Astro, the first dog created from the gene bank after the Invasion, right on to contemporary dramatizations of the lives of Hildy Johnson's bulldog, Winston, and Sparky Valentine's Bichon Frisé, Toby.—PC

(BTW: In the category of dog movie classics, Sherlock is a big fan of Pluto, but thinks Goofy is kind of creepy, even scary. His thoughts on Goofy would translate as "What the fuck is he?" I agree with him.—PC)

I do not like taking baths. But when αChris takes me to

the groomer I like the smell of the other dogs there. I can tell who has been there in the last five or six days. There is a nice groomer there named Alice. She is gentle with me and never gets soap in my eyes. I would like to hump her leg, but I have learned that humans do not like that.

(Leg humping is another example of dog humor.—PC)

Sometimes I wish I had hands like humans. I could throw my own balls and chase them! Not my ass balls, but balls for throwing like tennis balls. Ha-ha! But then I remember how slow humans are, and I know that dogs are the best possible animal. No one could improve on CEC dogs. Then I feel sorry for humans, who cannot smell for shit. But I get over it.

I like meat. Any kind of meat, but ground dino is the best. I like vanilla ice cream. I like Bowser Bow-wow's Bacon-flavored Doggie Snacks. I like cheese puffs, especially if they are extracrunchy. I like broccoli. Other dogs think I am crazy to like broccoli, but I do. Fuck them.

I still have my balls. αChris says I can keep my balls as long as I am a good dog. He is joking. I think. I am always a good dog anyway, just in case. I like to lick my balls. I like to lick them even when they do not need licking. I like to do it when αChris is with someone else because it "embarrasses" him. Ha-ha! I do not understand what embarrass means, but I think it is funny the way he smells when he is embarrassed. His skin grows damp. He smells of hot sausage. I think αChris would lick his balls if he could. I think all humans would lick their balls if their spines were not so stiff, except for human bitches, and they would probably lick themselves, too. Why not?

(If you have ever seen a dog, you will know that they have no sense of modesty or embarrassment. They don't care what they do or what they look like or who sees them.—PC)

Well, that is me. As you can see, I am a good dog, and I am very smart. I like the way Miss Penelope Cornflower smells. She does not smell like corn, but she does smell of certain types of flowers. Since I met Miss Penelope Cornflower I have been 'facing with her to tell my story of what happened to αChris and me. So I will start now.

Any mistakes in the telling are her fault, not mine.

————————

The bitch blew into our office like the stink of things rotting on a sandy beach. αChris has taken me to a sandy beach in a disneyland called Hawaii. I liked running on the sandy beach but I did not like to get too close to the water. There were rotting dead things on the sandy beach. I liked the smell of them. I was not so sure I liked the smell of the bitch. Maybe I would like her smell better if she was among the dead things on the beach. Bitch on the beach. Get it? Ha-ha!

(And with that joke I will cease referring to females as bitches. I know it is the term breeders use, but many people find it offensive, including myself. Male dogs are not romantic, neither normal ones nor CECs. They do not fall in love, they do not wish to start a "family," they merely get the urge to have intercourse. From then

on it us up to the females in the pack to tend the young. Very much like some dedicated human males if I may venture an editorial opinion!——PC)

I knew at once that there was something wrong with her. I knew I had to investigate. I got up from my comfortable rug and ambled over to where the female was sitting. I sniffed at her glove and smelled something I had never smelled before. This was very interesting to me. I filed the scent away where I keep such things in my mind. It was related to certain things I knew that were like putrefaction, but it was not the smell of the dead. This was even more interesting. It was a little like some stinky cheeses, and a little like sweaty gym socks that have not been washed in a while.

With a few more sniffs I was able to learn more things about her.

For one thing, when she told αChris that her name was Mary Smith, I could smell the lie. The lie smelled like heated metal and garlic.

I could also tell that she had had a shrimpoid cocktail with extra horseradish for lunch, and a salad of bibb lettuce, radishes, croutons with Parmesan cheese, lemon juice, olive oil, pepper, and crushed anchovies. She had washed it all down with a harsh red wine. I do not like wine. I like a bowl of beer now and then.

(I am never totally sure if Sherlock is showing off or pulling my leg. But I suspect he would not kid around with smells. Smells are serious business to Sherlock.——PC)

I could also tell that "Ms. Smith" had been in heat two or three days ago. Human females come into heat a lot. She had also taken a shit not long before she came to our office. She had no hair in her armpits or in her pubic region. I do not know why humans shave off their hair. Hair is good.

(Sherlock did not use the term "pubic region." I thought it best to tone down his rather rougher image.—PC)

I decided that was enough information for now. I could do a more detailed examination of her later if αChris wanted it.

I returned to my rug and got comfortable. I am not nearly as lazy as αChris thinks I am. I patrol our apartment at night, investigating interesting sounds. I sometimes go out and snoop around while he is sleeping. I just close my eyes when life gets boring. I daydream, but I am not asleep.

I kept "one ear open" to listen to them. That is a human expression, one ear open. Humans often say things that are not real. I am still learning how to tell when they are doing that. I like it when they do that, most of the time. It tickles my mind in a pleasant way as I try to figure out what they are really saying. But sometimes it is confusing.

"Ms. Smith" wanted us to find someone. I like finding people. I am very good at finding people!

She took off her gloves. I opened one eye to see what I already knew. The ends of her fingers were missing. And I heard a word that described what had happened to her. "Leprosy." I filed it away in my scent file.

I was not sure of what I was hearing, but it sounded like

someone had given her the disease. On purpose! What a bad person! When I found him, it would be very hard to stop myself from biting him. Hard. In the balls. I have never bitten anyone in the balls, but I have thought about it. I think I might enjoy it if it was a bad person.

I have only bitten a human once, and he was a very bad person. I liked biting him. But it was not in the balls. It was on his ankle. I tasted blood. The man was hitting me on the head, but I did not let go until the police came and carried him away. I like to think about biting that man as I am going to sleep. I dream about it, too. Does that make me a bad dog? Just in case, I have never let αChris know about it.

"Ms. Smith" said the man who poisoned her had a blister on his mouth. I would remember that and keep my nose open for the smell of a blister. There are different kinds of blisters. I wanted to see what kind of blister this man had and take a good sniff of it.

"Ms. Smith" was becoming upset. I could tell from the tone of her voice and from a smell of a kind of fear. There are different kinds of fear. Each smells different. All fear smells intriguing. When I smell fear something exciting is usually about to happen.

Then αChris got out his bottle of poison and poured some into glasses. αChris thinks I do not like the smell of bourbon poison. This is not true. There are no bad smells. Bourbon is a powerful smell, and that is interesting. But I do not like to see αChris poisoning himself. Sometimes he poisons himself into a stupor, or sleep. This is not good for him. When I smell him the next morning, he smells of sickness. I am thinking that αChris may be an "alcoholic," but I am not sure of this yet. I will think on it some more.

I left our office. I could still hear them clearly through the wall.

"Ms. Smith" said she thought I was beautiful. This showed she was intelligent because I *am* beautiful. I decided I did not dislike her as much.

αChris said my name was Watson. He does not want our clients to know that his partner is a dog even though I am a CEC and very smart. I do not mind this. One of the principles of private detecting is to "never show all your hand." That is another expression that is not real. I do not have hands.

I wished they would talk more about me, but they went back to telling and learning about the case. I was a little sad to hear αChris say we would not harm the man when I found him. My partner does not believe in violence except in self-defense. I am never quite sure what self-defense is, and I sometimes want to bite a bad person because biting him would feel good. But I do not bite him.

"Ms. Smith" said she would like to tear the man's balls off. I liked her even more. But she would be satisfied with taking the man to court. Court is a place where humans are taken when they have been bad. Then they are put "in the doghouse." That is another joke. Ha-ha!

They talked for a while about things that confuse me. They spoke of a virus. I have learned that there are tiny animals that live inside us. Humans and dogs, too. They can make us sick. I do not know if they live in cats or birds or fish. I hope they live in cats. I do not like cats. I hope the kind that make you sick live in cats. I am not sure I believe these little animals are real. I have wondered if αChris is "pulling my leg."

Then they talked about money. I do not have much use for money. I have a credit chip in my collar. αChris keeps it stocked with "walking around" money in case I want to buy something. I would prefer "running around chasing a ball" money. Ha-ha! I bought a ball once. I took it to a park and found people to throw it for me. Some people will do this, and I do not even have to reward them with a Bowser Bow-wow Bacon-flavored Doggie Snack. Ha-ha-ha!

———————

After "Ms. Smith" left, αChris got up and asked me if I wanted to play our game. Does a damn cat shit in a box? We race each other to see which of us can get home first. I always win, which is the best kind of game.

αChris usually goes part of the way on his bicycle, then puts the bicycle and himself on a train and gets off one stop short of the escalator to Noirtown. Sometimes he takes a slightly different path. I have trailed him several times, and I know all of his tricks.

He knows that I must take a train to keep up with him. He does not know where that train is. He has never gone underground to look for it. I sniffed it out long ago and learned how to ride it. I will not say how to get to this train, not even to βPenny. A dog has a right to some secrets.

(I'm glad that Sherlock finally started thinking of me by the name Penny. That's what everyone calls me. I don't mind that he regards me as a beta female. That's what I am.——PC)

I was ahead of him that day, too. Ha-ha!

He grabbed his hat again and went out. I stood and waited until I could not hear his feet going down the stairs, then I hurried back out the door and down the back stairs. There is a dark alley back there. I scratched at an alley door, and my friend Whitey opened it and let me in. He scratched my ears, and I licked his hand. Then he tossed a ball of raw dinoburger into the air, and I snagged it. Good boy, Whitey! That's a good boy! Ha-ha.

Whitey went back to cooking his "blue plate specials." I do not know why he calls them that. They are always different, and the plates are not blue. The food is not blue. Today the blue plate special was Hungarian goulash. I smelled onions and lard and garlic and carrots and . . . was that parsnips? I have never eaten parsnips, but I have smelled them. Tomatoes, mild green peppers, hot red peppers, potatoes. And . . . caraway seeds, paprika, eggs, and flour. Wheat flour.

Whitey put a bowl down on the floor and ladled a portion of the Hungarian goulash into it. I like Hungarian goulash. I scarfed it all down. αChris thinks I should eat slowly and taste each bite carefully. Why? One of my other early memories is being crowded out at the bowl by other puppies. It is a dog-eat-dog world out there. Ha-ha! If you do not grab what you can, who knows what will come along and swipe your portion?

There is a space between the Nighthawk Diner and the building next to it. I can get there by squeezing behind a machine. When I pressed my head to the wall I was only a short distance away from the booth on the other side of the wall. I could hear αChris talking to someone.

I quickly realized it was γHopper. I do not like γHopper. His eyes when he looks at me are full of hate. He smells of old cheese and civet shit. I do not mind the old cheese, but I do not like the civet shit. I would very much like to bite γHopper's balls, but I have not. So far.

αChris calls Hopper a "two bit grifter." I do not know what two bits is, but I have learned that a grifter is someone who tricks someone else and steals their money. This makes me angry. It makes me want to bite Hooper's balls even more. Maybe his dick, too. A dick is a penis and also a detective. I am a detective, but I am not a dick. That is a joke. Ha-ha!

I listened to everything αChris and Hopper talked about. I did not understand all of it. They talked of sickness. I was sick once. I threw up and made a mess. I tried to eat it again, but αChris told me not to. He said it would make me throw up again. He said I ate a "bad clam." I know what a bad clam smells like now. I would not eat a bad clam again.

αChris said there were people who were making other people sick. If that meant the people were feeling the way I felt when I ate the bad clam, then those people were very bad. I wanted to bite them all over. The balls and the dick would be just the beginning!

Then αChris said one word. The word was "Irontown." I had never heard that word before. Then his voice changed. He sounded afraid.

I was not afraid. I would follow αChris into Irontown if he went there. I would guard his back and fight with anyone or anything that scared him.

I would not be afraid.

t's probably impossible to draw a logical connection between being Chief of the New Dresden Police and running a dino ranch. But that's Mom for you. She seldom
does what you might expect her to.

She was always busy, as police chief, keeping the citizens
of New Dresden safe in their burrows. And she was good
at it, I'll give her that. She was the one responsible for de-
fusing the only nuclear bomb to ever threaten her city. She
did not have much of a life outside the police department
and, oh yeah, raising me when she had time for it, between
frequent sixteen-hour workdays.

Everyone was surprised that, when she retired from
her job with a pension that meant she would never have to
work again, she really never worked again. Never set foot in a
police station. She retired to her little empty cylinder deep

under Mare Imbrium, where I grew up. It was fairly distant from the city. She was devoted to breeding extinct reptiles.

That was the plus side of growing up with a mother who was usually too distracted by her job to be around to give affection and encouragement to her single human puppy. I always had plenty of pets to play with. Usually had a few bite marks on me from the more rambunctious of my carnivorous playmates.

———————

To get to the Rockin' New-Moan-Ya Ranch you had to take the express tube to Pythagoras, then double back almost a hundred miles on a local. The ranch is an unscheduled stop, so don't forget to inform the driver or you'll shoot right past it.

You get out in a small station that contains not much but a freight port for large shipments. Then you ride it down several miles until the door opens, and you get a faceful of the distinct odor of dinosaur shit.

Mom's cylinder is not huge, nothing like a disneyland or a pocket environment. It's about a thousand feet in diameter and two hundred feet high. You needed that much room for Tiny.

Tiny is possibly the largest animal in Luna. She may be the largest animal that ever lived, on Earth or Luna that is, though there is no way to be sure. The biotechs who first reverse-engineered her genome were surprised at the longevity of some dinosaur species. Tiny is fat and happy at a hundred and forty-six Earth years old, over one hundred and sixty feet of spotted *Argentinosaurus huinculensis*, the Great Antarctic Titanosaur. Her neck alone is almost eighty feet. She is forty-five feet tall at the shoulder. She eats every waking minute. She has to, to maintain her sheer bulk. She doesn't seem to mind.

Mom inherited her when she bought the breeding ranch. She didn't want her, but there was no choice. Tiny had long ago grown too big to be moved in any reasonable way.

Tiny is always on the alert for visitors, who arrive on a wide ledge at a point about a hundred feet up the cylinder. This is not a bad stretch for Tiny's immense neck. She has never shown aggression, even to strangers, and with those she knows, she trumpets loudly and stomps over from wherever she had been cropping and—I sometimes think—contemplating truth, beauty, and infinity. Well, you can't prove she isn't.

Tiny did that now as soon as she spotted me, galumphing along with her head held high. She laid her head on the ledge beside me. That head was about the size of a two-person rover, which sounds big, but is ridiculously small for an animal that enormous. She nudged me with her cheek, and I had to catch my balance.

There was a bin against the back wall, with a lid that showed a lot of teeth marks where Tiny had tried to pry it open. I went to it, and her head followed along behind me.

I pulled the cover open and took out . . . well, what would *you* feed a dinosaur? Tiny likes several things in addition to her daily diet of ferns, seaweed, and other greens. She will take pineapples or watermelons, but her favorite is coconuts. I grabbed an armload.

"Open wide, Tiny."

She did, and I lobbed two in at once. She cracked them like I might have cracked a sesame seed. I guess she likes the taste, though she would have to eat them by the bucketload if that was all she had. But I guess you could say the same for elephants and peanuts.

When I was younger I was forced to operate the small bulldozer we used to shove her poop into the composting bin. Now that task is accomplished by a robodozer, as, of course, it could have been all along. That was Mom for you, using a very direct lesson to prove to me that I should get a good education. Otherwise, you could be doing something like this for a long time . . .

I didn't take any more convincing.

———————

I went through the air lock to the other part of the cylinder, the smaller part where the breeding animals are kept. This lock was for more than emergency backup in case of a blowout. There were flying creatures in this part of the habitat, and if one of them got loose, it was much easier to recapture it in this part of the cylinder than in Tiny's world.

Mom used to breed land dinos like miniature stegosauruses and triceratops, no bigger than poodles or even Chi-huahuas. Now it was all flying reptiles.

Pterosaurs came in all sizes, from the gigantic Quetzal-coatlus probably the largest animal that ever flew, with its thirty-foot wingspan—to the Tapejaridae family, which includes Nemicolopterus, the smallest pterosaur ever, about the size of a finch.

And unless you are a breeder or collector, you probably don't know those species names. Nemi-etcetera is better known as a flit in your neighborhood pet store. I don't know why. Others are known as scalykeets, though they are not scaly, or repticopters.

I had to pass through the aviary to get to the lab, where I figured I would find my mother. Cages of various sizes held single specimens or flocks of the smallest flits.

There's always something going on in the aviary. Pterosaur squawks and hisses don't sound much like bird-songs, and frankly, several hundred of them all crying out at once sets my teeth on edge. I used to wear earplugs.

This is the business Mom had wanted me to go into. She was strongly opposed to my following in her footsteps, becoming a bobby or a cop, or—who knows?—maybe chief of police, like her. I told her I had handled enough dinosaur turds to last me a lifetime and soon I had my own beat.

It would have been a lot better if I had stuck with prehistoric-reptile ranching, but who knew? The Glitch was something no one saw coming, least of all yours truly.

———————

I found Mom in the hatchery. It's dark in there. It's warm, too, maintained at a constant thirty-eight degrees, which seems to be the temperature the eggs like best.

Mom was examining a rack she had just pulled from one of the incubators. Ptero eggs vary in size from baseballs to not much bigger than a jelly bean. Most of them are leathery before they are opened, though a few are hard calcium, depending on the diet of the species.

The embryos in the rack she was examining were tupandactylus, one of the largest species she bred. A full-grown tupan has a wingspread of around five meters, and stands as tall as an average human when on the ground. They were called "sailboat" pteros, because they had the largest crests relative to their size of any of them. The crest of a mature sailboat could be three meters high and two meters wide, as large as the rest of its body excluding the wings. And the crests could be colored in an array of oranges and reds, sort of like the wings of an outrageous monarch butterfly. Add in the huge red beak that seemed to be adapted for cracking nuts, and you had a perfect ornament to any rich citizen's menagerie. I don't think there are more than a few dozen of them in Luna.

———————

I leaned over and kissed the top of Mom's head.

"Hold on a minute, Chris," she said. She had never

glanced at me as I entered, but she always knows when it's me.

People meeting my mother for the first time are often surprised by how tiny she is. Even standing on her tiptoes, she can't quite make it to five feet. So this is the legendary Anna-Louise Bach?

You bet. And I'd advise you not to mess with her. She has studied just about every martial art there is for a hundred years and could take you apart without breaking a sweat. If she had to, she could kill you with just her fingernails. It is hard to believe that such a tiny person could have gestated and delivered a big lug like me, but she did.

I looked over her shoulder at the egg rack. There were a hundred developing embryos, each in its egg-shaped depression and covered with a clear plastic layer. They were at the stage of their development where it was half critter and half yolk. They still weren't moving around much, but every once in a while you could see a twitch. The wings had just started forming. The heads already had long beaks, which they would normally have used to cut through the leathery shell. The eyes were huge.

"Pick the worst one," Mom said. I slowly ran my eyes over the sleeping nightmares.

"Six down and four from the left," I said. Mom reached for a forceps and plucked the little creature out of its incubator and tossed it into a bin on the floor.

"Not the worst one, but definitely not show quality."

That was as high praise as Mom would usually give out.

"This one is the most promising," she said, pointing to a baby that looked completely identical to all the others.

"Good to see you again," she said, grudgingly. "You don't come around often enough." There was a pregnant pause. "So how are you feeling, Christopher?"

That translates as "are you about to have another breakdown, or are you just your normal, fucked-up self?" She no longer bothered to comment on my trench coat, gray fedora, and black leatheroid shoes, all of which were not often seen outside of my habitat. If I needed to dress up to keep my tenuous grip on sanity, that was all right with her.

"Okay, and I'll try to get here more often." It was a lie, and I'm sure she knew it, but she accepted it. She stood on tiptoes, and I leaned over for her to plant a motherly kiss on my cheek.

Mom's living quarters are at the far end of the ranch property, so I had to follow her through the rooms where hatchlings were grown to full-size, ready-to-ship juveniles. The pathway was lined with cages containing all the species Mom breeds. Some of them were very large, up to thirty-foot cubes, and some were more suited for a single canary.

We came to the door to her domicile. She let the door warden scan her eyes. The lock clicked open, and we went through, then through the second door and into her parlor. It's a comfortable place of no particular style, pieces assembled haphazardly as she found the need for something. She went to the bar in the corner and fetched some glasses.

"Where's Sherlock?" she asked. Sometimes I think she

likes my damn dog more than she likes me. I can't blame her, actually. Sherlock is more likeable.

"I left him to run in the Free Park. I'll bring him next time."

"Do that." She crossed the room and handed me a tumbler with a single ice cube and some homemade vodka, strong enough to raise the dead. It's all she ever has. I took a careful sip, she took a gulp, and we settled in overstuffed chairs by the fireplace.

"So what's on your mind?"

"Irontown."

She actually flinched. You didn't see that often with Chief Anna-Louise Bach, but Irontown and the Big Glitch were an awful memory to her, a reproach to everything she stood for.

MORE WAGS OF SHERLOCK'S TAIL

wanted to get moving on our Irontown case, but it can sometimes be hard to get αChris to get up off his lazy, tailless butt. I have learned that I cannot nip at his heels. Whining does no good. And I do not like to whine, anyway. Whining is for puppies.

So we wrote a lot of tickets to smelly people. I have had to learn which smells are okay and which ones are bad. Every dog knows there are no bad smells, but humans insist that some are bad. I do not think humans, even αChris, know that I and other dogs *like* the smells of stale sweat, old piss, the many things that can waft from head hair and crotch hair and fur, and any kind of shit. They are all interesting smells. The world would not have much flavor if those smells were not in the air!

But I do like finding the smelly people and picking them out of a crowd. I like it even better if they run. I wish they might turn around and try to fight with me, so I can bite them. When I am chasing someone, my back is up, and I am ready to fight. *Grrrrr!* When I say that, they get frightened. I can look frightful when my back is up. *Grrrrrrrrrrr!!!*

They almost never try to fight.

I have said that though I love αChris as much as life itself, he can be very stupid sometimes. When Mary Smith left the office, I wanted to follow her, but I am not supposed to do that on my own. I thought about doing it anyway, but I did not. I wish I had followed her.

Then he should have had me scent her the next day, or the day after that. It would not have been easy, but I am a very good scenter. But it was three days before αChris asked me if I could trace her. I wanted to bite him. Just a little bite, a little nip, to tell him he had done something dumb.

I started in the lobby outside our office. It was easy to pick up her scent there. She had been there for a few minutes, and there is no wind blowing through the lobby. There is a grill near the floor where air is sucked in. There is a grill near the ceiling where air comes out. I sniffed them both. She had not come or gone through the grills. I did not think she had. I could smell that the ducts behind the grills were dusty. Mary Smith had not had dust on her clothes when she entered the office.

I pawed the button for the elevator, and we waited. When it opened I went inside. I could smell her there. It was the slightly bitter, slightly juicy smell of her leprosy. It is a stronger smell than most humans have, except for the stenchers we track down and arrest. I was going to go down in the elevator with αChris, but then I sniffed again. The trace in the elevator was a little older than the one in the lobby. I came back out again and followed a trail to the stairway door. This trace was a little older than the one in the elevator. So she had gone up in the elevator, then walked down the stairway. Elementary, dear Sherlock!

(Mr. Arthur Conan Doyle made a movie called *The Hound of the Baskervilles*. Mr. Basil Rathbone took the role of Mr. Sherlock Holmes, my namesake. I do not like this movie. The hound is killed. He was half mastiff and half bloodhound, so he must have been a relative. I would like to glow in the dark like the hound did, but I do not think I would like to be painted with phosphorus. I do not know what phosphorus is. I have never smelled phosphorus. αChris says it is nasty stuff. He says it would burn my nose. I do not want my nose to be burned.)

Her spoor continued all the way down the stairs and out into the ground-floor lobby. There it became fainter. There it became mixed up with other smells. I was able to follow it outside and into the mall. In the mall I cast around and thought I could follow her a short distance in the direction away from our home. But I was not sure, and before long I lost even that faint trace. This made me sad because I do not like to lose a scent. I sat down and looked up at αChris. He patted my head and said he was sorry that he had not had me on the trail sooner. This made me feel a little better. I would not tell him he was stupid.

I did not want to tell of my visit to the home of the mother of αChris, but Penny says I should. So I will.

I do not like the mother of αChris, whose name is γAnna-Louise. She does not like me, either. I do not like the animals she keeps in her home. I do not have much use for reptiles other than to smell them and their shit, which is interesting. γAnna-Louise breeds dinosaurs. The dinosaurs she breeds are the kind that fly. Some are no bigger than squirrels. I like squirrels, but I do not like dino-squirrels. Some are as big as flycycles. Some are even bigger than flycycles. I do not like these, either.

The dinosaur I do not like the most is called Tiny. Tiny is a titanosaur. Tiny is very, very stupid. Tiny spends all her time eating. I think she even eats when she is sleeping. I have learned that cows chew their food again and again. I think this is very interesting. I would like to see this happen some-day. I think Tiny chews her food again and again. She eats plants. She is too big and clumsy to catch squirrels or rabbits, so she has to eat plants, which are slow. One time when I was with αChris visiting γAnna-Louise, Tiny tried to eat me. She picked me up with her mouth. I was very frightened, and I cried out in fear. I did not like to cry out like a puppy, but I could not help myself. Tiny's mouth smelled interesting, like water that has been standing and has frogs living in it, and like sulfur and wild onions. I wondered if this was going to be the last thing I ever smelled. This made me sad. I did not want this to be the last thing I ever smelled.

γAnna-Louise hit Tiny on the head with a big stick. Tiny's brain must work very slowly, because she stopped lifting her head, and a moment later she dropped me. I am glad γAnna-Louise hit Tiny on the head with a stick, but I still do not like her.

Tiny is too old to have a pack. All her pack died away many, many years ago. Maybe a shitload or even a double shitload of years ago. I feel sad for Tiny because of this. No being should be without a pack. But I still do not like her. If Tiny did have a pack, I think she is so stupid that she might be a θtitanosaurus in the pack, or even a letter I do not know of. αChris says that the last letter is ω, omega. I think Tiny is probably an ωtitanosaur.

αChris knows I do not like to go to the dinosaur farm and so he told me to stay home. I know I am supposed to obey αChris, but when we are on a dangerous case like *The Case of the Leprous Dame of Irontown* I do not like to let him go off on his own. He is likely to get into trouble, and I need to be there to keep him safe. So I let him stumble down the stairs in the front of our apartment and listened for the slam of the door. Then I was up and out and down the back stairs.

Now is when being a very smart dog, a Cybernetically Enhanced Canine, comes in very handy. I have small devices in my head. I do not understand what these devices are, but I have always known how to use some of them. I have learned to use others. One of these devices I think of as a mouse. It is not a mouse, but that is a good way to think of it. This mouse can find the tiniest cracks to crawl through. These cracks are in the security machines that let people in and out of doors, or do not let them in or out. Most dogs are not allowed through doors without their masters. I can go through most doors.

I wear a beautiful collar all the time except when I am taking a bath. I do not like baths. This collar has shiny steel spikes in it, so anyone trying to bite my neck had better look out! But inside this collar is a device that calls out to doors and tells them to open. I cannot turn doorknobs or pull on handles. Sometimes I can push against a door to open it, but I do not need to. The device calls out to doors, and they open for me. Only CEC dogs have collars like this. Only smart dogs like me.

But the mouse is different. I have heard humans talking about programs. Some of these programs are called worms and some are called bots and some are called apps and some are called viruses. They are not really worms. They are not really viruses. I do not know what a bot is. An app is what is left after you have eaten part of an apple. Ha-ha! I like apples but would not like to eat them all the time. Unless there was a Bowser Bow-wow's Bacon-flavored Doggie Snack inside. I must ask αChris to make me an apple with a Bowser Bow-wow's Bacon-flavored Doggie Snack inside!

With my mouse I can walk or run through a world I do not really understand. It is like the map I have in my head. This is not a map I have made myself, because it shows buildings and streets and alleys and ducts where I have never been. But it is very clear. I think this is an app that someone has put into my brain. It is a map app. Ha-ha!

I can think of a place I want to go and the map app will show me a way to get there. I have learned that most humans have an app like this in their heads. This makes it easy for them to get around. I can see a path in my eyes. I have learned that this is not a real thing. It has no scent.

αChris does not have a map app in his head. This is because he is afraid someone will take over his mind. I do not understand this, but if αChris says it, it is probably true. Probably. Most likely. Possibly. But it makes αChris very slow and clumsy. If he did not have me to lead him to where he wants to go, he would always have to ask people for directions. He says this is what he used to do, before we became partners. He got lost a lot.

When I think about the mouse I find myself in a strange land that I do not understand. There are no scents there, so I do not love it, but I have found that it is very useful.

(Sherlock was very reluctant to tell me about this strange land

*of his, and I can see why. I don't think anyone else is aware of just
how much he is able to do in the cyber world. Because what he is
describing is clearly some sort of access to digital realms where he
really has no business.*

*(I did a little research and as far as I can tell he is not able to
cause any real mischief when he goes sniffing [so to speak] around
in the virtual world. And yet, no one realizes he can do the things
he has clearly done, either. I will say more on this later.—PC)*

One of the things I learned that I can do in my strange
land is go places where no one can really go. I have not gone
to many of these places yet because they frighten me. I am
a brave dog, but this place worries me a little. That is because I cannot lay down a scent trail. When I turn around
and try to go back, I cannot always easily see where I have
been.

One of the places I visited was the inside of my collar.

Oh, I am so confused! It is not really the inside of my
collar.

Perhaps Penny can explain these things.

(I'll take it from here, Sherlock.

*(I am not notably cyber-savvy myself, other than the everyday
knowledge we all get in school and through life experiences. But
apparently he has accessed the programming of his collar. It seems
that he saw a virtual image of his collar and walked his virtual self
into it. Once there he was able to intuit that certain codes could be
changed. Without really knowing what he was doing, he repro-
grammed his collar to open a lot more doors than it was originally
intended to open. This opened vast new vistas in his real world. It*

enabled him to constantly surprise Chris Bach by his ability to show up in places he could not possibly have reached. This is how he was always able to beat Chris home from the office.

(As I said, Sherlock did not want to talk about this. He is afraid that if anyone learns what he can do, he will be forbidden to do it. I join him in this worry. I doubt that the authorities would be thrilled to learn that a mere dog is able to circumvent so much of their precious security. Few of them would realize that, in his own canine way, he is much smarter than they are.

(So we reached a deal, dog to human. I will keep this information under strong security until he gives me the okay to reveal it. This extends even to Chris, which was a painful and hard decision for Sherlock. We agreed that the story needs to be told in its entirety, in view of . . . but I'm getting ahead of myself. Back to Sherlock.——PC)

When αChris goes to visit his mother he takes a train all the way out to a place called Pythagoras. Then he has to take another train some of the way back until he gets to a small stop that almost no one ever uses. On my first trip to the ranch this is the way we went. But my map app told me that there is a quicker way.

I left our apartment warren and hurried to the nearest air duct. It was only a short way down the corridor. I looked around to be sure no one was watching, and then I told my collar to tell the grate to open up. My collar pretended it was a maintenance robot, and the very small brain that controlled the grate believed my collar. The grate was very stupid. It opened with a springing noise. I went inside. It

74

was a duct that a human could have crawled along on hands and knees. Since I was a much more sensible four-legged dog, I could run as fast as I wished.

It was windy in the duct. I liked the wind because it brought many interesting scents. I wanted to explore them but I ignored them because I was hot on the trail of a case. I followed my map app to an intersection of more ducts, then through a noisy place of fans. Finally I reached a place that hardly smelled of humans at all. It was an intersection where many machines came together and were sorted out by other machines I could not see. My map app told me where to get aboard a train car. The train car was not as comfortable as the train cars humans rode in. It was hard and clattery and not very clean. I sniffed it out thoroughly as the train started up, then settled down on the floor. I wished I had my comfortable blanket to lie on. But when I am on a case, I do not mind discomfort.

My collar told the train to slow down and stop, and I got off. I knew where I was. The next door I went through took me to a room just beyond the big room where Tiny the Stupid Titanosaurus was chewing her cud. I could smell her even through the shut door. I liked her smell, even though I do not like her, and even though it made me scared. A little.

I found a place to hide behind some sacks of dinosaur food. It was not food for Tiny. It was food for the ugly little flying dinosaurs that γAnna-Louise raised. She sold these ugly little dinosaurs. I do not know why anyone would want to buy one. They look too scrawny and bony to be worth eating. I wondered if their bones were like chicken bones, which smell good, but αChris says are not good for dogs to eat. He says a dog could choke on them. He is αChris, so he is probably right. Maybe. I will think more about this. Food is food.

The dinosaur food in the sacks smelled good. I thought about tearing one open and eating some. But that might give away that I was hiding behind the sacks. So I did not tear one open. Besides, maybe dinosaur food had chicken bones in it.

I curled up on one of the sacks where no one could see me. It was even more comfortable than my blanket back home. Maybe αChris would get me a sack of dinosaur food to sleep on. I tucked my nose up under my hind leg and went to sleep. I usually sleep when there is nothing else to do.

———————

I woke up when αChris arrived on the elevator from the train stop. My map app said the stop was a long way overhead. I held still until he had passed into the room where Tiny the Stupid Titanosaurus lived. If αChris had been a dog, he would have smelled me. Humans cannot smell for shit. They can barely even smell *shit*. Ha-ha!

I told another air duct to open for me and followed my nose to the place where γAnna-Louise keeps her flying dinosaurs. I crept up on another grate but did not tell it to open. I could see a little through the grate. I could smell much more. I smelled many kinds of flying dinosaurs. I could hear the awful squawks they made. I smelled eggs, but they were not bird eggs or turtle eggs like we eat at home, though they smelled a little like turtle eggs. I was very interested. I would like to eat some of those eggs. Maybe when we solve *The Case of the Leprous Dame of Irontown* αChris can steal some dinosaur eggs from γAnna-Louise.

I saw αChris walk by and I moved along the air duct with him. He had passed through the aviary into the hatchery. There the smell of eggs was even stronger. I licked my lips. The two of them talked for a while about breeding flying dinosaurs. It was very boring. If they had talked about if they were good to eat, I would have paid attention. But they did not talk about that, just about how to select the best eggs. I could have told them that with one sniff. I like eggs.

Then they moved into the last rooms of the dino ranch. This was the apartment where γAnna-Louise ate and slept and pissed and shit and fucked. She had eaten something with pasta in it a few hours ago. Pasta and sausage. I licked my lips. I like pasta and sausage. Her piss and shit smelled healthy. She had not fucked in those rooms for a long time. I could still smell the flying dinosaurs and the dino shit, but not as strongly.

The grate here was higher up, and I could not get to it. But I could hear them. γAnna-Louise asked why I had not come. αChris told her he had left me in the Free Park where I was happy chasing balls from the automatic ball thrower. This was a lie. He had not left me in the park. γAnna-Louise told αChris to bring me along the next time he visited, and he said he would.

In your dreams.

They sat down, and I heard them pour glasses of poison to drink. I could smell that this was the clear poison known as vodka, not the brown poison known as bourbon. Poison is poison. Except for beer. There is only a little poison in beer.

Then αChris told her he was there to learn about Irontown. And I could smell the fear that burst out of her skin.

eight _____

My mother had never talked about her involvement in the big raid on Irontown that resulted from the Big Glitch. It was such a fiasco that I assumed she had spent the intervening years trying to forget all about it. But of course she couldn't. It wasn't her fault; all the investigative committees convened afterward agreed with that. She was exonerated. But in the only evaluation of the raid that mattered to her, she was guilty. And that was the court of inquiry in her own mind.

What I had hoped for in my visit was to pick her brains about Irontown itself. As someone who had been high up in the planning stage, I figured she knew things that might come in handy for me.

It turned out she did. But first, to my amazement, she wanted to talk about the raid and the Big Glitch itself.

"I was the one who suggested the operation," Mom said, taking another hefty belt of her moonshine. "That damn place was a blot on the city, on the damn planet, even."

"Technically, Luna isn't a planet," I said.

"Don't get technical on me. You always did that, even as a child."

She glowered at me. Relations between me and my mother can be strained at times.

"I wanted to clean it up. Clear out the squatters, liberate the area, bring it all back into the civilized world."

I didn't point out that "liberating" would not be the word the squatters of Irontown would have used for the operation. More like "invading." Or maybe "evicting," or "terrorizing."

"One warren at a time, that was my original plan. Stretch it out over maybe a year, maybe even two. Take one neighborhood, clean it up, empty it out, and make sure no one could get back in. Then move on to the next one. Use a small force of handpicked officers, give them extra training, even some paramilitary courses to make sure we showed up with overwhelming force. One of the cardinal rules of police work."

She didn't need to tell me that. She often seemed to forget that I had been a cop, too, once upon a time.

"It was that goddamn mayor," she went on. "Up for reelection, needed to do something that would get on the news feeds and show the voters he was actually doing something while in office. He wanted it quick and dirty and, above all, 'cinematic,' as he put it. He didn't quite have the nerve to say he actually wanted violence, but it was made clear to me that no one would really mind it if things got bloody. No deaths unless the eyecams would show clearly that the officer's life was in danger.

"He couldn't just fire me, he'd have to go to the council, then get it approved by the CC. But he could make the job just about impossible if I didn't give him what he wanted, so I gave in."

She brooded about that for a moment. Took another belt.

"Hell, I'd meant to go in with nothing but stun pistols, happy gas, and dragnets, but found myself issuing projectile weapons. We had to get out the manuals just to learn how to use them. And it took another month of range practice before any of my officers could hit the floor without shooting off their own feet. I never did get very good at it."

"You did the training, too?"

"I decided I had to go in with my troops. If they were going to have to do it, I wanted to lead from the front, not the rear."

My mom had balls. I'll give her that.

"Of course, no one knew at the time that the Central Computer was behind it all. I mean, *naturally* we knew the CC was a part of the raid. Back then, it was a part of *everything*. And we never even thought about how vulnerable that made us all."

She took a third—or was it a fourth?—belt and scowled. I thought about prodding her but decided to wait it out.

"Next thing I knew, I was in nominal charge of the biggest paramilitary operation in Luna since . . . hell, since maybe ever."

Once more she lapsed into silence. I found I was actually holding my breath. Anything at all might break into her mood and send her right back to the silence of the past. But she still went on.

"I don't know at what point my leadership became just titular. Nominal, like I said. The mayor was the guy the public saw, the one who planned to get all the glory for cleaning the place out. I was to be the brains behind the operation. Just part of my job.

"Only I began to realize, as the thing snowballed and started careening out of control, that my participation was going to be marginal, or maybe even nonexistent.

"And one day the real soldiers arrived, with authorization straight from the CC itself. Big, ugly, nasty fuckers recruited from the dregs of Pluto and Charon, who didn't take orders from anyone but the CC.

"I don't mean to whine about it. I made a lot of mistakes, the biggest one being my failure to resign when I saw how it was going. In my defense, I never saw just how bad it was going to get, or I would have refused the order to start the raid. But I should have refused anyway. I guess in the end I was just too chickenshit to do it."

"If you knew it was going to go bad, and went ahead

anyway," I said, "then that would be true. But you couldn't have known."

"The signs were all there. I was being paid to see things like that. But thank you for saying so.

"There was one other reason I didn't speak out. I was afraid that the raid would take place anyway, and if the Irontowners would have known what was coming, they would have had time to prepare better defenses than what we were planning for."

She suddenly threw her glass across the room. I was startled. Outbursts like that were not Mom's style. I'd seen the slow burn often enough, growing up, but seldom the explosion.

She put her head in her hands, and for a moment I thought she was crying. Which would have been a first, in my experience. Then she looked up at me and slowly shook her head.

"Irontown, Heinlein Town, who knew the difference? I didn't even know about the Heinleiners until two days before the raid. And, of course, it turned out that's what the raid was all about. The CC had it in for the Heinleiners, they had something the CC didn't have, and that was intolerable to our big, friendly AI brain. The null field. The thing that made it possible for those fuckers to go without a pressure suit!

"Our maps were shit! The CC itself wasn't sure where ordinary Irontown ended and Heinlein Town began. I couldn't have cared less about the rest of Irontown. Let those rejects from society go their way in peace. But the

Heinleiners were different. They weren't losers, and they weren't stupid. They were voluntarily separating themselves from society not only because they found it too restrictive but because of a paranoid theory that we had put too many of our eggs in one basket, so to speak."

She frowned.

"Paranoid," she huffed. "Who knew that they were the only ones in Luna who were *right* about the CC?

"If I had it to do all over again, I'd leave the Heinleiners alone. They weren't bothering anybody but the CC. Sure, they were breaking the law, or some of them were, anyway, but as far as I can tell, they were being extremely careful with their genetic experiments."

Once more she stopped and steamed silently for a moment. Then she relaxed. Or maybe it would be more accurate to say she slumped.

"It was out of my hands at the end, anyway. The CC placed those mercenaries from the Outer Planets Coalition, those 'sergeants,' those combat veterans . . . placed them in charge. I was forbidden to even talk to my own cops, the ones who had been selected for the raid."

"Then they can't blame you for what went down," I said.

"True. They never blamed me for it."

But it ended her career. She saw what was coming and resigned before they could find a good reason to fire her.

"That's all, Chris," she said. "I can't talk about it anymore."

"Sure, Mom," I said. "Here, let me get you another glass, and we can have one more drink before I go."

It was the perfect opportunity for me to tell her about *my* experience of the Big Glitch. But like a dozen perfect opportunities before, I let it go by. I wasn't sure I would ever tell her.

Did she need another load of guilt? No. But was she entitled to know what happened to her only child on that horrible day?

The jury was still out on that one.

———————

Mom had never been one to share her thoughts and hopes and memories and all that heart-to-heart stuff. Her one great fear was to be seen as weak, so she cultivated the tough exterior. I was the only one who knew that beneath that hard shell . . . was another shell, just as hard.

It turned out that although she had heard of the fad of engineered "harmless" diseases and other disfigurements designed and intended to be disgusting to the general population, she didn't know much about it.

"Before my time," she said. "But it's just like any number of other fads, I'll bet. One of the things Irontown was always about was nonconformity. I understand every generation has things they do to flaunt their independence in the faces of their parents." She glared at me over the top of her glass. I don't know why. I had always been a good little girl as a child. When I decided, at the age of twelve, that I preferred to spend most of my life as a male, I was an obedient teenage boy. I didn't hang with the "bad" kids, didn't do anything to spite my mother. Could she have been disappointed in me because I *didn't* rebel? That would be just like her.

"The most extreme rebels have gone to Irontown in the last four or five decades. It's a fashion that just stayed around longer than usual. There have always been enclaves . . . I think the word is 'bohemian' . . . There have been places for artists and misfits and people who wish to isolate themselves from the larger society."

Her eyes lost focus for a moment, and I knew she was accessing data with her neural implant.

"Paris in the nineteenth century. A place called Greenwich Village in New York City in the twentieth. The Rocks in Sydney in the middle of the twenty-first. Places where people could band together and sneer at all the people who didn't think like they did. There's always been a bit of that in Irontown, along with the criminal element."

That was a major concession from Mom. I had never heard her say a good word about the place, or even a neutral word. "Irontown" was a word she always spat out, like she didn't want it to linger in her mouth.

"Leading up to the Invasion, there was a major fad for body modification," she went on. "Again, it started in primitive cultures, with scarification, piercing things like earlobes or noses. Some cultures stretched parts of their bodies, like lower lips."

"How?"

"You know they didn't have anything like modern surgery. The modifications hurt, and the only way to stretch skin was to stress it over a long period of time."

"Did they *like* pain?"

"There have always been people who want to be hurt, but it's usually a sexual thing. I think the pain of tattooing and body modification was part of the rite, something you had to endure. I suspect that if they had the technology we have, most of them would have elected to avoid the pain. You know that childbirth used to be horribly painful, don't you?"

"So I have heard."

"You could *die*. Sometimes the contractions lasted days."

I frowned at her.

"Do you think . . . I mean if you had to go through that . . . would I ever have been born?"

She laughed and took another swallow of her joy juice.

"Not really a fair question. Hypothetically . . . probably not. I don't like pain any more than anyone else. But I told you before, I wasn't even sure I wanted a baby at all for a long, long time. But having made the decision, I welcomed you into my life."

She probably really saw it that way. And it wasn't entirely untrue, it just overlooked a lot of things.

She shook her head, looked vaguely disoriented. I sensed we were about three sips away from unconsciousness.

"Oh, right, body mods. The fad started somewhere in the depths of the twentieth century with simple piercing. Just about anything you could poke a hole through without dying, like nipples and labia and penises. Some pierced their tongues, which must have been exquisitely painful."

"Not to mention the penis."

"Some went further. They split the penis in half. Don't ask me how those men pissed. I don't know, and I don't want to know."

"I wasn't going to ask."

"Good. Of course those sort of things are pretty common these days, minus the pain those people must have endured. But if you go to Irontown you'll see things more radical than that."

"So . . . when you were setting up the raid, did you encounter any disease mongers?"

"I don't recall any involuntary cases. That's what you're asking about, isn't it?"

"Yes. I have a client who was given something that's turning out to be hard to get rid of."

"You know how she got it?"

"That's what I'm trying to find out for her."

She scoffed. I wasn't sure if that was over the foolishness of M. "Smith" for getting infected, or at me for taking the job. She has quite a low opinion of my line of work, which

I guess is traditional for a cop. In the books, the flatfoot is always threatening to take the license from the shamus.

I had just about concluded that it was a wasted trip—except of course for the pleasure of seeing my mother and scratching Tiny's enormous nose—when she raised her eyebrows a little, which I knew from past experience was the sign of a lightbulb going off in her head.

"'Ever'body go to Mistah Scrooge, 'cause Mistah Scrooge, he know ever'thing an ever'body.'" She blinked and burped.

"And that means . . . what?"

"Excuse me. Mister Scrooge is Mister Big in Irontown. At least he was back when I was chief, and I see no reason why he wouldn't still be the man to see."

"What was that, some sort of slogan?"

"Excuse me. Yeah, something like that. You go to Irontown and try to find out anything, that's what they will recite to you."

"So you think I should go there and ask around for Scrooge? Walk into a bar or something, start buying drinks for people?"

"No, I do not think you should do that. First . . . excuse me . . . first, you shouldn't go into Irontown or Heinlein Town or Steelville at all. You're just not equipped for it, my darling child, no matter how tough you think you've become from reading all those stories."

I didn't think I was that tough at all, but I had to put on some sort of front or I just couldn't cope. Which she knew.

"You're . . . you're not quite right in the head, Christopher, and you know it."

"Mom . . ."

"Don't you deny it. Just look at you. Those ridiculous clothes, that hat, that silly dog that follows you—"

I got up and doffed my stupid hat at her.

"I won't hear Sherlock insulted, Mother, not even from you. I'm outta here."

"Sit down, Christopher. *Sit down!*"

I sat down. When my mother used that tone of voice, hardened prestupniks have been known to fall to their knees, sobbing and confessing their crimes. I was able to resist that, but not the command to sit down.

"Okay, I'm sorry I insulted your dog. You know I love that flop-eared goofball. Where is Mr. Holmes, by the way? He's usually with you."

"Last time we visited, Tiny tried to pick him up. Remember?"

"Oh, yes, I forgot. You know Tiny just wanted to play."

I knew Tiny hadn't intended to eat Sherlock, being a vegetarian and all, but try telling that to a dog who is about to disappear into that huge gullet. No, I figured that from now on if Mom wanted to pick him up by the ears (which he loves, by the way), she would have to come to him.

"All right," she said, "I'll accept that you are going there in spite of my advice. So let me give you some more. Do *not* go asking around for Scrooge. He has ears everywhere, and he is the most paranoid individual I've ever known. He doesn't exist in any database, which is so difficult to do these days that I doubt there are more than a few dozen people in Luna who have accomplished it. Outside of Heinlein Town, of course. Those folks have been evading all databases including the CC for decades. So it's impossible to confirm or refute his claim that he remembers the Invasion."

Well, *that* startled me. It's been a long, long time, and so far as I know the lineage of the Founding Families is all accounted for.

"That would make him . . ."

"The oldest living human, yeah. I go back and forth on whether it's the truth or not. Longevity treatments were pretty primitive back then. And you have to take into account that he is an accomplished bullshitter, too. But I do know he is very old."

She took one more belt of moonshine and, this time, suppressed a belch. I figured she was now one sip away from oblivion.

"So if I don't go around asking where to find him, and he doesn't exist in any database . . . how do I contact him?"

"Let me emphasize this: Definitely *do not* ask about him. People have been known to disappear if he thinks they are a threat to him. Think of him . . ." She looked thoughtfully at the ceiling for a moment. "Think of him as like a boss of the Charonese Mafia."

I hoped she was exaggerating, to scare me. If she was, it worked. I won't pretend that those words didn't make the hairs stand up on the back of my neck. It would have that effect on anyone who knew anything about them. The Charonese Mafia were legendary pirates, assassins, torturers, and just all-around blue meanies. They were said to eat their young, disrespect their mothers, chew up steel plates and spit out bolts, kick puppies, and not flush the loo after taking a dump.

Okay, I'm being facetious, maybe because making a joke about them helps to keep the actuality of them at arm's length. It's whistling past a graveyard, whatever that old expression means.

I don't think most people could point to Charon on a chart. It's a place good folks will never visit, so why should they clutter their minds up learning about the awful place? But I had done a little reading on the subject some years ago, and almost wished I hadn't.

Charon is the largest of Pluto's moons. If you think of Pluto as a good substitute for the Biblical Hell, which I do, Charon is the bottom circle. For a long time it was the place where Plutocrats, and some Martian, Titanian, and Cerean courts dumped their most incorrigible criminals. Transportation seems to be an irresistible urge in the human race. Ship them off somewhere and forget about them.

I understand that the descendants of transportees to

Australia, which was a country in Earth's southern hemisphere, were just like anybody else. Crime was no more prevalent down there than it was anywhere else. I also know that many, if not most, of those who were transported were sent for ridiculous offenses like being unable to pay bills. It wasn't a population composed solely of child rapists, mass killers, bomb throwers, and the like.

Not so in Charon. You had to fuck up in spectacular fashion to get a ticket to that miserable ball of super-cooled ice.

Since none of the Eight Worlds practices capital punishment, the minimum requirements for survival were provided. There was already plenty of water there, and power from the cryogeysers and cryovolcanos that litter the moon. Oxygen was dropped to the prisoners for some years, but later it could be obtained from hydrolysis of the water on the surface. Burrows were dug and basic tools and raw materials were provided for hollowing out more tunnels, on a much smaller scale than we have on Luna. Finally hydroponic farms were established, so the outside world could stop dropping rations. What I read was the prisoners subsisted on beans, broccoli, apples, chicken, and vitamin supplements for decades, until the orbiting prison guards relented a little and sent them other things to grow. You might expect that people would get a little grumpy on a diet like that, and you would be right. You could not have designed a better environment to breed people with little to no moral sense. There were no laws, no rules, no guards, no warden. Escape was impossible. It was pure Darwinian selection, where the strongest rose to the top and the weakest died. The most powerful bred. The rest . . . masturbated, I guess.

So, you put all these ingredients together and let them simmer for almost a century. About fifty years ago, we stopped transporting criminals. Since they were self-sufficient, "civilized" society turned its back on the inmates completely. Out of sight, out of mind. And good riddance.

Until the Charonese built a primitive spacecraft and landed on Pluto, about seventy years ago. It was a big surprise, but it shouldn't have been. A lot of the technology needed to stay alive at all on a barren rock like Charon or Luna could be used to evolve better machines, just as happened on Earth before the Invasion.

It was a big dilemma. What to do with them? The crew of ten had been carefully selected, all of them descendants of transportees. None of them had ever been convicted of anything. The "ambassadors" claimed that there was a government on Charon, and they wished to be admitted to the Eight Worlds (which by then was a lot more than eight worlds, but the name stuck) as a full member. They wanted full rights to travel to any of the other worlds, even seek immigrant status there, just like any other citizen.

There were some who worried about them, but many more who sympathized with their plight. The final word was spoken by the Interplanetary Union Court. Charon was to be admitted to the confederation as a full member.

It wasn't long before most everyone who knew about them regretted that decision. But since they deliberately kept a low profile, most citizens were only vaguely aware of the viper we had taken to our bosom.

"Scrooge is not Charonese," Mom said, bringing me back from my distasteful reverie. I realized I was a little drunk, too.

"I just used that as an example to get your head turned in the right direction if you deal with him. Which I say again, you shouldn't."

"You know I'm going to try. If I can't nose around and ask questions, what would you recommend as a way to contact him?"

"With a hundred-meter pole would be nice. With him at the wrong end of a shotgun would be nice, too."

She sighed and leaned forward toward me. She started to speak, then stopped herself and actually looked to the left and to the right, searching for hidden listeners, something I had only seen before in movies where an actor is playing a crazy paranoid. Apparently satisfied that no spies were lurking behind a giant fern, she started again.

"I must be out of my head to tell you this, but maybe it will save your life. I won't bother to swear you to secrecy, but I'm commanding you to never tell anyone what I'm about to tell you. Only three other people in the world know this, and two of them are dead.

"You were a cop long enough to know what a confidential informant is, right?"

"A fancy phrase for rat."

"Squealer works, too. For many years, and including the planning for the operation in Irontown, Mister Scrooge was my mole. He fed me information. I met with him twice, and I know how to get in contact with him."

When faced with an unpleasant chore, there comes a time when one must gird one's loins and spring into action. When it is time to fish or cut bait, to get moving, hie thee hence, step on it, turn on the steam. Hit the ground running, bestir oneself, get the lead out, buckle down, get the show on the road, look lively, shag ass, shake a leg. Shit or get off the pot. Carp that old dime.

So I managed to waste one more afternoon by making up that list of ways to say stop procrastinating.

Up to that point I had managed to waste a week getting very little done. Sherlock and I wrote up a lot of body-odor and environmental-stench tickets. He loves doing that, but I suspected that even he was getting impatient for me to get going to Irontown.

I hadn't told him yet that he would not be going.

If I had really been on the ball, I would have followed her from the office or, better yet, set Sherlock on her tail. But I really hadn't expected her to be that hard to find.

As an ex-cop, I still retain access to some policing tools. By using some friends still on the force, I was able to expand those tools beyond what a reservist would normally be able to access. I was able to gain access to the stored camera data through my contacts. Beginning the search for Mary Smith cost me the price of four dinoburgers. Extra mayo and hold the jalapeños.

I downloaded what I needed to start out, and FFed through a lot of nothing happening to her arrival outside the office. Sherlock and I watched it several times. The only thing we got from it turned out to be just about the only clue we had to follow. For a moment, after stepping off the elevator, she lifted her veil and applied some sort of cream on her ravaged skin. We never saw her whole face at one time, but that was easily solved. In the handy-dandy private-dick kit of programs I bought from an old hand at the game, I selected one that could take all the fragmented images of her face and put them together like a 3D puzzle. When it was done, there were a few blank spots, but the program found it very easy to fill them in.

I had to look away from it after I had studied it for a few minutes. There seemed no way to tell what she had looked like before the disease began to work, and what she was left with wasn't nice to study. Sherlock kept looking at it, though, and did that sniffing thing he does when he wishes humans had invented a process of smell-o-vision. I don't think he's even aware that he does it.

There are apps that can take a skull and interpolate what the face had looked like. It turns out this works for disfigurement, too. The program took a few minutes of chewing over the data before it delivered a three-dimensional bust that floated in the air over my desk. It turned around slowly. There was no expression on the face.

Sherlock put his paws up on the desk and watched as the head rotated. He sniffed a few times, then returned to his blanket. I had the feeling he was dubious.

In the old detective novels, the writer usually would insert a description of the dame here. Her best features would be scrutinized by the private dick. Eye color, breast size, complexion, shapely legs encased in sheer nylon. Her clothing would be itemized, from her low-cut blouse to her bright red high heels. She would always be a stunner and either given to sultry looks or showing signs of distress.

In my world, anyone who wants to be a knockout broad, in terms of twentieth-century ideas of beauty, can *be* a knockout broad. It's all up to you. This can lead to a certain sameness of face and body. If a person from 1950 were to show up in Luna in my era, he might have a hard time telling one of us from another.

There are nonconformists. Some prefer to look older and wiser. Some like to accentuate some feature, like very sharp cheekbones or a larger nose. A certain percentage don't really give a damn and present to the world the face and body that our genes dictated at birth. Naturals.

A police report on an individual in the age of Philip Marlowe would include many things that are variables today. Myself? Okay, I'm an average-looking guy, slightly taller than the norm. Hair: brown and slightly unruly. Eyes: brown with flecks of yellow. Body type: somewhere between ectomorph and mesomorph.

But there the police report ends, and even that data is subject to change. Distinguishing marks? Seldom any scars unless the person uses one as a beauty mark, and that could be gone by tomorrow. Today, most people decorate their bodies from time to time, but they use photo-creams and project the art onto themselves. It washes off with another cream.

I could have wished that Mary Smith was a natural, but no such luck. There was nothing I could see that was really unique to her. I was pretty sure I could have picked her out of a lineup, but maybe not if I just encountered her on the street. I wouldn't quite say the reconstruction was a generic pretty female, but it was close. There was nothing that really caught the eye, no unique mark you could hang an ID on.

Well, if it were easy, there would be no need for private eyes. Of course, Mom says there actually *is* no need for them. Gotta love a supportive mother, don't you?

The next step was to track her from camera to camera after she left my office and the Acme Building. I thought it would be a piece of cake, and again I was wrong.

Catching her coming out the front door was easy enough. The opaque veil made it a cinch to track her for the first five minutes or so. She walked confidently through the crowd, back straight and head held high. She looked in shop windows, reversed course a few times, and now and then stopped and looked casually around. I frowned as I followed her. There was something going on here that I was missing. When I figured out what it was, I mentally kicked myself because it should have been obvious. She was looking for a tail. She must have thought it possible that I would be suspicious of her and try to follow her home.

I don't claim to be the world's greatest shadower. She probably would have spotted me. It's a lot harder than it sounds in the books, believe me.

Which means I should have sicced Sherlock on her. He never gets spotted, because he can trail somebody and stay completely out of sight.

Apparently having assured herself that there was no inexperienced shamus dogging her heels, she then changed her behavior. She walked a straight line, more or less, no looking behind, no doubling back, no watching for reflections in window glass. But she was looking up a lot. And as

I switched from camera to camera as she went out of and back into range again, several times she seemed to be looking right at me.

She was spotting cameras.

What the hell was her game? Why would she care if I knew where she was going?

I got the distinct feeling that I was being played, and I had no idea why. When you find that you are in a different game than you thought you were, there's only one wise thing to do, in my opinion. Stop playing. Take your paddle, your net, your Ping-Pong table, and your ball and go home. Either I would never see her again, or she would show up and ask me why I wasn't working for her, in which case I would be sure to learn a lot more about Ms. Mary Smith before continuing in her employ.

That would be the wise thing to do, no question.

I knew I couldn't do it.

It wasn't so much that I knew none of my fictional heroes would do such a thing, though that was part of it. I mean, what would Elvis Cole say? I'd be drummed out of the Diogenes Club.

No, it was that I had developed a taste for the chase. Even though I knew most of my cases were the modern-day equivalent of finding a lost cat or collecting a bad debt. I really wanted to find this doll.

So I kept at it, and soon was even more certain that she was running some sort of game on me. She ducked into a public restroom.

It is one of the few zones of privacy left in our society, other than our own homes and the offices and surgeries of doctors and medicos. And, of course, it is a cultural relic from past days, the taboo about photographing someone in a toilet. It dates all the way back to the time when public restrooms were labeled MEN and WOMEN. Or LADIES and GENTS, or POINTERS and SETTERS. These days it's impossible to define, so they are just single rooms with toilet stalls and urinals. Silly or not, no monitoring is allowed. So Mary Smith was out of my sight for about ten minutes.

I think Sherlock sensed my frustration. He raised his head from his fifth snooze of the day and slouched over to the screen. We both watched as I FFed through those minutes. Finally here she came, presumably having done her business.

Now she marched straight ahead, looking neither left nor right. It was easy to keep her in sight, as she never deviated. She entered a residential compound, one I wasn't familiar with but which was just a standard habitat, nothing out of the ordinary.

And Sherlock began to get restive. He made a low *whuffing* sound deep in his throat. Then he made it again, then looked at me dolefully. Okay, a bloodhound's expression is always sort of doleful, but this was even more gloomy than usual. He put his head back and let out a howl. I don't think I have heard Sherlock howl more than three or four times in our five-year relationship. Clearly, there was something he wanted to tell me.

It is at times like this, and *only* at times like this, that I wished I had an implant in my brain that would allow me to interface directly with my canine partner. Still, we have always worked it out before. It's like a game of twenty questions, but it usually takes no more than five.

"Okay, Sherlock. You're upset. Did you see something?"

"Arf!"

Damn. I wasted a question. *Obviously* he saw something. I didn't need his disdainful look to tell me that.

"Okay, sorry. Is it something she did, or didn't do?"

He shook his head sharply, his big ears making a flapping sound. Wrong question. Hmmm.

"I'm stumped," I admitted. "She hasn't done anything but walk straight ahead, then go into her habitat."

"Arf!"

"Yes? She went into her habitat?

"Arf arf!"

"No. Hmmm . . . well, she walked around for a while."

"Arf!"

"Well, sure she walked. What else was she going to do?"

To my surprise, the recording started running backward, rapidly. I hadn't done anything. Was it some sort of glitch? The playback went into forward again, and Sherlock put both paws up on the desk and actually pawed at the screen. He looked over at me, imploringly.

I watched her walk. Damn it, it was just a woman with a dark veil, walking. What was so interesting about that?

Then I saw it. The walk was all wrong. Well, not *all*

wrong, or I would have spotted it, too. Now, I wouldn't say that everyone has a walk that is unique. There aren't an infinite number of ways to move along on two legs. The walk I was seeing wasn't *radically* different from what it had been when she entered the restroom. But it was different enough.

"She ditched us!" I shouted.

"Arf arf arf arf arf arf!!!" Sherlock was chasing his own tail in his excitement over having pointed this out to his dumb master.

Sometimes I wonder if Sherlock thinks I'm pretty damn stupid.

———————

Later, we watched the video outside the apartment where the bogus Mary Smith had finally gone to ground. It must have been a pretty large place because over the next few hours, we saw several dozen men and women enter and leave. No one that we saw was sufficiently close to the imposter's walk that we could be sure it was her.

But first there was just no stopping either of us from hurrying to the place where she snookered us. Yes, us, because she fooled Sherlock for a while, too. And yes, she fooled me longer. And yes yet again, she probably would have fooled me forever if not for Sherlock. I'm not above giving a dog his due. I might still be staked out outside the apartment waiting for her to come out if not for his keen eye.

We raced down the stairs, and I started off at a jog, which of course was not nearly fast enough for Sherlock. But a trolley came along, and I flagged it down. The conductor rang his bell, and we were off.

"The game is afoot!" I cried to Sherlock, and he licked my face.

———————

We stormed through the restroom door and looked around. It was a fairly big space, and smelled okay to me, with just the slight pong of disinfectant. It had been days. Would there still be a trace of her?

Sherlock snuffled here and there, back and forth. I could see the world narrowing for him as he took in huge snoutfuls of air. He had attracted an audience, people who had been at the sinks and were now watching him work. I think they could sense his intensity.

"Is he after a fugitive?" one man asked me.

"Let's just say a suspicious character," I said.

This spread a sense of excitement among our audience. It's not often that a melodrama intrudes into our real lives.

Sherlock could not have cared less. I watched him carefully move around the room, and then as he was drawn to a ventilation grate at the back of the room down near the floor. He sniffed it a few times, then sat down and looked back at me.

"She went through here?"

"Arf!"

I knelt and examined the grate. Totally standard, about a meter wide and a little less than that high. I could see where there was a catch that would open it for servicing, but I didn't know how to operate it. It probably needed a pass code of some kind. I pushed my hat back on my head in my frustration.

"I don't think we'd learn much even if we could get it open," I told Sherlock. He lifted his left forepaw and scratched at the grate in what looked like frustration. He scratched again, and the grate popped open with a twanging sound.

Even without a cyber interface, there are times when I can read Sherlock's mind perfectly. He looked at me, and said, "Well, why didn't you try it to see if it was *locked*, idiot?"

"Sherlock, you're a genius." I opened the grate and stuck my head in. Nothing much to see but dust on the bottom, and in the far distance in either direction, small spills of light that I assumed came from other grates leading to other rooms.

"Can you still smell her?"

"Arf!"

And he shoved past me and took off down the air duct.

ten _____

SHERLOCK AGAIN

did not know if αChris would wonder why the moving pictures we were watching of the Mary Smith who was not even the fake Mary Smith suddenly ran backward. I do not think other dogs can lie very well, and I do not think they are tricky. I am learning to lie and be tricky. I am very smart and I am very good at many things. But not that.

I finally managed to make him see what I had seen, that this was not the Mary Smith who had gone into the place where humans piss and shit in water. I would not like to piss and shit in bowls of water. I like the pissing posts and dirt patches around the city. I can smell who has been there recently.

If I could have smelled the fake Mary Smith, I would

have known at once that she was not the original fake Mary Smith.

We went to the piss-and-shit place where she went in and did not come out. I soon picked up the faint traces of her scent. It was not easy, but I am a very good scenter. The trace was strongest by the air duct, so I sat down and looked at it.

I went to that place in my head where I store the things I stole from the places outside my head where such things are stored, and I found the signal that would open the grate. I scratched at it and it opened. I worried that αChris would think I had opened it by thinking about it, but he didn't.

(And why would he? When something strange happens around you, is your first thought that your dog probably did it? I had to laugh.—PC)

He thought I had opened it by pawing at it. I think this was a clever thing for me to do. I am still learning how to be clever.

As soon as the grate opened, I hurried into the duct. I quickly knew in which direction she had gone. I started running that way.

"Sherlock, come back!" αChris said.

"Arf arf!" I said.

"What do you mean, no?"

I wanted to tell him that I just meant that I wanted to stay on the trail but I do not know how to say that to him. There are many things you cannot say by barking once for yes and twice for no.

"You just wait a minute," he said, and got a thing out of

his pocket that showed a map. I looked at it and saw that a little shape that looked like a dog was blinking off and on, off and on. The little dog thing, which I have learned is called an icon, did not look like me at all. It looked like a poodle. I do not look like a poodle. I would be unhappy if I looked like a poodle. Why do people trim poodles that way?

"This is you," he said. I sniffed at the thing. "This shows where you are. This thing is too low for me to go very fast, so I'll let you go, but you can't go far. Okay?"

"Arf!" I said. I took off as fast as I could.

Not very far away the scent stopped. I was by another grate. I looked back and saw αChris looking down the duct at me. He had a small light that he had taken from his bag that he called his ditty bag. I do not know why it is called a ditty bag. I have never seen anything called a ditty and I do not think that αChris keeps any ditties in the bag. But he keeps many other things in there. Sometimes these things come in useful.

"Is that as far as the trail goes?" αChris asked.

"Arf," I arfed.

"I'm coming down."

The duct was just big enough that αChris could walk on his hands and knees and his back did not scrape the top of the duct. Humans are very bad at walking on four legs.

When he reached me I thought I might have to open the grate myself, but he felt around the edges of the grate with his hands. He swung the grate away from us and started to crawl through, and I crowded in beside him.

Then there was a shriek. I looked up and saw a woman looking scared as she looked down on us. I pulled my head back, and a hot wokful of General Tso's chicken landed on αChris's head.

———————

After αChris stopped howling I tried to help by licking the places where he was burned. I did not know he could howl like that. It was good General Tso's chicken, but it was not really chicken. My nose told me that it was bronto chunks. I have learned that bronto chunks are cheaper than chicken. I like both bronto chunks and chicken, but neither of them are as good as Bowser Bow-wow's Bacon-flavored Doggie Snacks. If the Bowser Bow-wow company made Chicken-flavored doggie snacks I would try those, but I think I would like bacon better.

———————

I knew αChris was hurt. I did not know how hurt. But it upset me. And then the woman who threw the General Tso's chicken on αChris was throwing bunches of bok choy and chunks of tofu and a bowl of rice and a bowl of water chestnuts at me. I do not like bok choy or tofu. Water chestnuts are all right and I will eat rice if there is nothing else to eat.

But I do not think she was trying to feed me. I dodged as well as I could, but I was backed into a corner. I thought about biting the woman, but αChris told me to stay. So I stayed. αChris told me he could not see very well. His eyes were swollen shut. His face was very red. I tried to lick off more of the hot chicken but αChris said it hurt. I did not like to see him hurt, and I thought about howling. But I did not howl.

Then the bobbies came and they wanted to tie αChris's hands together. I growled and snapped at them. I knew I should not snap at them, but I could not help myself. They backed off when αChris told me to be quiet, then they helped him stand up.

There was a lot of talking then, and I didn't listen too much. I just wanted to be sure no one was going to put the things on αChris's hands. I have learned that the things were called handcuffs.

Someone said he had decided he would not press charges. I did not know what that meant, but αChris stopped smelling worried, so I knew that pressing charges would be a bad thing. αChris offered to pay for the damages and the food the woman had thrown at him. I do not know why he would want to do that. Humans do not eat off of the floor, usually, and so they thought the food was ruined.

I do not understand why αChris would pay for ruined food. I thought of eating it myself, but I found out that I was not hungry. I was full. In fact, I was about to pop, which is something I heard αChris say once when he had finished a big meal for Christmas. Christmas is a day for eating until you are about to pop. On Christmas we eat strange things like cranberry sauce and a bird called a turkey. I think cranberry sauce is okay. I think turkey is very good.

I like Christmas. I do not know why we do not do it more often.

———————

Some people came and put αChris on a bed that had wheels under it. I followed along beside them until we reached the mall. We both got into something called an ambulance.

I had never taken a ride in an ambulance before. The ambulance made a terrible howl, and people got out of the way. For some reason, I could not stop myself from throwing my head back and howling along with the ambulance. I do not know why. The people inside the ambulance and αChris made that barking sound humans make when they think something is funny. The word for it is laughing. I do not know why they thought it was funny. I did not think it was funny, and I am a dog who likes jokes.

———————

We got out at a hospital. A hospital is like going to the vet, but for humans. I do not like going to the vet, but αChris says it is good for me. He says it will help me live longer. I want to live longer, so I put up with it. But I do not like it when the vet pulls back my lips and looks at my teeth. I really want to bite her. But I do not.

The human vet did some things to αChris's face, and to some places on his arms and chest that were red and smelled burned. Before long the redness of the burned places went away, and αChris said he felt better now, and we could go.

I was happy to leave. The smells in the hospital were very interesting, but they made me nervous.

We went home and αChris threw away the shirt that still had some General Tso's chicken on it. I sniffed at it for the last time, and I wondered who General Tso was. He must have liked ginger, garlic, soy sauce, sesame oil, and vinegar. I do not like any of those things all by themselves, but in General Tso's chicken they taste okay. I do not know why they taste bad by themselves, but okay when they are cooked. I will think about this tonight.

Then αChris said that healing burns took a lot of energy. I did not know what that meant, but I could see and smell that he was tired. I was tired, too, and about to pop. He changed into his pajamas and got into bed.

I do not know why humans put on different clothes to sleep in. I do not really know why they wear clothes at all unless it is cold. But it is never cold in the city. It is cold in the Alpine disneyland. αChris and I went to the Alpine disneyland once. I liked the snow. I liked running through the snow beside αChris as he slid down a hillside on boards called skis. I did not like walking or running on ice. I could not stand up. Then αChris gave me some boots that stuck to the ice. I do not like boots, but it is better than sliding around on the ice.

When αChris began to snore I curled up on my rug. Thinking about snow, ice, cooking, chicken, Christmas, hospitals, and the way Mary Smith smelled, I went to sleep.

The next day we went back to the place where αChris was burned. I learned that it was a restaurant, which is a place humans go to have someone else cook their food for them. The name of the restaurant was the Lucky Loonie Double-Happiness No-MSG Garden.

I know what a garden is. It is a place with plants and flowers and dirt where you are not allowed to piss or shit. I know what happiness is. I do not understand what luck is. I went to the place in my head where I can ask about things, and the answer was that No MSG is a word meaning "all-natural ingredients." Sometimes when I learn what a word means I don't really know any more than I did before I asked. This was like that.

The manager of the Lucky Loonie Double-Happiness No-MSG Garden was a small man who did not look happy to see αChris or me. I was not happy to see him, either. He was the one who said he would not press charges. αChris again offered to pay for the trouble we had caused. The manager held out his hand so they could do the thing humans do by pressing their thumbs together to exchange credits.

αChris has told me before that people are often surprised when he gives them "folding money" instead of thumbing them credits. Many people have never handled paper money, he told me. They are surprised that there still is paper money.

"Someday, Sherlock," he once told me, "they will outlaw real money once and for all, and I will be fucked." I understood that he did not mean fucking like sex, but fucked like "in big trouble." I like it when words mean two or even three different things.

αChris spends a lot of time worrying about being fucked. He also tells me about things that are fucked up. That means bad. Then there is fucking this and fucking that and fucking the other thing.

Fuck is one of the best words I know. It means so many things! Ha-ha!

The manager, who was named Mr. Freberg-Wong-Tong, told αChris to follow him to the kitchen. Then he said that I could not come. αChris gave him some more money, and we went to the kitchen.

There were one two three four five people in the kitchen, cooking things. One of them was the one who threw the General Tso's chicken at us. The manager talked to her, calling her "Pumpkin." I did not know this word but I have learned that a pumpkin is a large orange squash. I have tasted other squashes and I did not like them much. I would like to smell a pumpkin. This Pumpkin was not large or orange. She was small, even smaller than the manager.

Pumpkin looked frightened for a moment, then held out her hand. I smelled the back of it. Now I would always know when Pumpkin was near. But I still did not know what pumpkin smelled like. Ha-ha! She rubbed the top of my head and scratched me behind the ears. I knew then that she liked dogs. I can always tell. I licked her hand, and she smiled. I tasted sweet and sour bronto. I like sweet and sour bronto.

The reason we were there is because αChris hoped that I might still be able to pick up the scent of the *real* fake Mary Smith, not the *fake* fake Mary Smith. I could have told him that it was too late for that, but I wanted to give it a try, anyway. And I did. There was none of her in the air or on anything else I sniffed.

"Any trace of her?" αChris asked.

"Arf arf."

He looked sad. This made me sad, too. I wished I could pick up the scent, but even my wonderful nose has its limits. I wondered if we were at a dead end. αChris once told me that private detectives like us do not always solve their cases like Nero the wolf in his old books of fiction. I do not completely understand what fiction is. I do not know how something can be not part of the world. Or what humans call the *real* world. Is there more than one world? I have heard of places called Mars and Pluto. I think they are other worlds, but I do not know if they are real. And I do not know where they are. They are not on any of my maps.

If fiction is not real, does that mean that Lassie the collie and Toby the Bichon Frise are not real? I would be sad if they are not real. I will keep thinking that they are real. Why not?

I would like to meet Nero the wolf, though. I have never met a wolf.

(I decided not to interfere with Sherlock's rejection of the idea of fiction. As he said, why not believe that Lassie is real? Toby, the famous actor Sparky Valentine's Bichon, actually is real, of course, unless we are all characters in someone's novel. Ha-ha, as Sherlock would bark.

(I did tell him that there was no wolf named Nero, though, and that Nero Wolfe was a fictional person, a private detective. I had to look that one up. The books were written centuries ago and are rarely read now. Then Sherlock wanted to meet the big fat detective, so it's clear he still doesn't get the idea of fiction.

(Sigh. I should learn to keep my nose out of Sherlock's business.—PC)

The manager and Pumpkin made some noises at each other that I did not understand. It was not laughing, and it was not coughing, and it was not crying. It sounded like words, but I did not know any of the words. This made me nervous. I have learned that there are way, way, way beyond a shitload of words and that not all humans know all of them. But I had never heard so many words that I did not know.

I have learned that the manager and Pumpkin were barking at each other in something called Chinese. I have learned that αChris does not know Chinese words, either. I felt better when I learned that. I do not know why humans have so many words they cannot all understand. I thought I might think more on this, but then I decided I did not really give a shit.

After Pumpkin had barked at the manager for a while

the manager talked to αChris for a while, barking words that I understood. I know that as a great private detective I should have listened to what the manager had to say, but I was distracted by Pumpkin's offering me a small morsel like I had never seen or smelled before. It was almost the size of a chasing ball, but it had one two three four five six seven eight legs.

I have learned that the legs are called tentacles and the creature was called an octopus. After hearing so many Chinese words that I did not understand, I was happy to learn two new words. The octopus smelled of brine and tasted a little like a clam. I like clams. I am still thinking about the octopus.

So I did not hear what the manager was saying to αChris, but after he was through αChris was excited.

"Come on, Sherlock," he said. "The game is afoot!"

Which is what he always said when he was on the trail of something. Which meant that I was on the trail of something, too. Whatever it was, it would not escape from the detective team of Sherlock and Bach!

"Arf!" I said.

eleven _____

understand that, for the very oldest of us, the most important question you can ask them is "Where were you when you first heard of the alien invasion of the Earth?" I knew a few of the First Generation, but none of them well enough to ask them that.

For most of the rest of us, unless you are from Mars or Pluto, the question is "Where were you during the Big Glitch?"

Those words drop like heavy stones into my mind:

THE.

BIG.

GLITCH.

We all have our own stories about it, of course, and endless stories about the aftermath, which is still being felt.

Most of the people I've met who want to talk about it seem to think that their own personal experience of the Big Glitch would make an excellent article or movie. Once I get them to finally stop talking about it, I know even more certainly that their stories fall into half a dozen general categories, and there is nothing at all remarkable about almost all of them. We are all the stars of own movie, aren't we? For most people, the story was how scared they were while waiting to find out just how fucked we really were. Of how we tried to contact loved ones in a world suddenly, and largely without precedent, cut off from all forms of communication more sophisticated than shouting, and of how to survive it.

Sorry, folks, we were all terrified. Your story isn't special.

There are so many compelling stories of heroism that only the most extreme were ever deemed unusual enough to be dramatized. You have probably seen a dozen of them if you are the typical viewer.

I have seen none of them, but I'm not typical.

There are some stories that claim to take us deeper into the inner workings of the Glitch. Some of these stories have been published in one way or another, and a few have actually been dramatized. They mostly concern the people whose job it was to bring the runaway train to a halt without totally wrecking the thing. They tend to be technical, but for those who can follow the technology, they are said to be real page-turners. A few of these stories are even believable, or so I've been told. Again, I haven't read them.

The most popular of these accounts, and an almost totally nontechnical one because she is hardly more cyberliterate than I am, is the story told by Hildy Johnson, the former reporter for the *News Nipple* newspad. I gather that she claims a special relationship with the Central Computer that predated the Glitch by almost a year.

She believes she is one of the first people to get a hint that something was deeply wrong with the CC.

In her account, she tells of meeting with and becoming a member of the Heinleiners, that group of malcontents out in the Delambre Crater who figured so prominently in the disaster.

Remember how it all got started when the CC decided those rebels were a menace to the orderly society that it had been building for over two centuries?

How the CC secretly raised an army of psychopaths from mysterious military sources on Pluto and Charon, brought them to Luna, and had them train a larger force of irregular soldiers?

How the Heinleiners proved to be a lot harder to subdue than anyone had anticipated? How, in fact, they *won* the miniwar waged there in the junkyards of Delambre, in the shadow of the great, failed starship, the *Robert A. Heinlein*?

How they came out of hiding long enough to help restore order out of the chaos, then melted back into their wary isolationism?

Sure you do. It's one of the great urban legends of our time. Some of it, maybe even most of it, may actually be true.

I don't swallow it all, though. For one thing, you don't "join" the Heinleiners. It's not an organized group, to say the least. You simply choose to live out there if you don't like a lot of people around you.

For another, she describes technological advances that were sure to revolutionize our way of life. We were supposed to be on our way to the stars by now.

As you may have noticed, we are not. What's up with that?

Hildy herself admitted to being an unreliable narrator. She warned us that she would be deliberately changing some details of her story, and not just the names to protect the innocent. This was all to help keep the secrets the man she termed "Valentine Michael Smith" felt humanity was not ready for yet. She threw some red herrings into her personal mystery story.

Okay, I'll admit it, I read her book.

In spite of my resolution to pretend the Big Glitch never existed, never happened, I knew Hildy Johnson's story was the most thorough and most likely to be true of all the accounts out there.

I knew it because she had almost killed me there.

———

I really can't hold a grudge against Hildy Johnson, though.

The fact is, I was trying to kill her.

I really did kill her dog, and I'll always be ashamed of that. I hope Sherlock never finds out.

In my defense, I hadn't meant to kill the dog. I hadn't meant to kill anyone or anything. I had been told these people were a clear and present danger to all I held dear. The rule of law, for one thing.

But once more I've shied away from the main thread of my story. It's just that, if I am ever to talk about Irontown and what goes on there, I first have to deal with the Big Glitch and what I did during it.

Remember I spoke of "irregular soldiers?" I was one of them. And I marched as blindly into hell as generations of soldiers did before me . . .

In retrospect it's hard to figure how reasonable it all seemed at the time. I cringe every time I recall how easily I was duped into it all. And yet . . . it was the CC. It was that friendly voice you had been hearing since childhood. It was almost as if your imaginary friend, Harvey or Hobbes, had suddenly started barking orders like an old drill sergeant.

But I was the poster child for gung ho back then, all eager to set the world on fire, or at least warm it up a little. I envisioned a rapid rise through the ranks until, who knows? Maybe the post of chief of police was within my reach.

All the experts will tell you that if you possibly can, it's best to avoid the profession or art that your parent was very successful at. But it seems the compulsion is very strong. Even big success in your parent's field of achievement will have, as an end result, everyone looking at you, and saying,

"Oh, right, he's so-and-so's child." Rehab clinics are choked with the children of fame. So are funny farms.

I spent some time in a psychiatric unit, but not for that reason.

———

The CC definitely knew people, knew what makes them tick. As well he should, since he manufactured a different personality for every one of the millions of inhabitants of Luna. We all felt that we had a deep personal relationship with the CC. That was true, in a sense, as that part of his vast capacity really *was* focused on you, and you alone. So it was deep, and it was personal, but what it was not and never could be was special. Everyone had their own little corner of the CC's mind to call their own. It was about as unique as having a belly button.

When he came around recruiting, he knew exactly which levers to pull. I said I was gung ho? You bet, and the thing I most wanted to do was enforce the law.

Most of our laws derive from the premise that someone famously summed up as "Your rights end where my nose begins." We're not so much into turning the other cheek, so if you start something, be prepared to see the other party in court.

Anyway, when the CC summoned me to a meeting and designated it as being held under the highest security rating, the only bells I heard were no alarms at all, but more like the bells that ring in fire stations when it is time to get moving with no wasted time. And like a faithful Dalmatian, I climbed aboard the flyer and soared into the air, heading for the smoke.

———

We met down at the very lowest, bedrock level of the city. It was a place where you expected rats to scuttle, where water was actually dripping from the ceiling before winding its way to a dirty-looking drain in the floor. There were light fixtures overhead, but few of them were working.

The place didn't smell very good. I'm sure Sherlock could have identified the smells, but I couldn't, except to say they were musty.

There were faded and peeling posters on some of the walls. They were so old that I had little idea of what they were touting, except it seemed to be some political party I had never heard of. If they had been meeting down there, I would have assumed they were on the fringes, maybe even revolutionaries.

———

It was at that initial meeting that I and my comrades on the force got our first look at our leaders.

How to describe them? Very few people outside the Heinleiner enclave ever saw one. For many who did see them it was the last thing they ever saw. It was almost that way for me.

There is even debate as to what exactly they were and

whether or not they were all the same. They gathered up their wounded and dead—leaving us common grunts to our fate. The survivors took off for the Outer Worlds that spawned them. No one ever found any of them, and no government or company ever admitted any involvement.

The smallest of them were at least seven feet tall, and well over three hundred pounds, none of it fat. There had been gene tampering that was illegal everywhere but Charon and Pluto. Somewhere under all that bulk was the cherry on top: machinery, not unlike some of the wilder creations of fiction writers before anyone had ever constructed a humanoid robot.

Much or all of the bone structure in these cyborgs was made of titanium. The muscles had been augmented with carbon nanofibers, giving the monsters extraordinary strength.

Judging from the metal skull fragments that were found, their brains were on the small side. Not small enough to make them stupid.

They were either all male or neuters. I certainly could not have told you without asking one to drop his pants, and of course these days even that would not have been conclusive.

My take on them is that they were not about reproduction or sexual pleasure. They were about fighting and killing, end of story.

Any one of them could have crushed my head with one hand, just by squeezing it. This went a long way toward making me want to please them if the orders from the CC hadn't been enough. My fellow conscripts seemed to feel the same way. When one of the cyber-sergeants said hop to it, we all jumped.

We didn't realize that we were being sold a bill of goods, at least partly because we were already sold. Though Luna was not under attack, it was the concept of law and order that we were swearing allegiance to.

Hurray for law! Let's hear it for order! We will die, if necessary, to protect those twin beacons of freedom!

Well, theoretically, anyway. We all knew no one was going to die. Who could stand up to us with the Mighty CC behind us?

It was going to be a walk in the park.

———————

One more thing that should have raised alarm bells was the lack of preparation. Our training was what you might call cursory. We set out on three consecutive weekends. We skulked through woods deep in the Bavaria disneyland, shooting at each other, though no Heinleiners lived in the woods. We had guns that shot pellets that stung quite a bit if they hit you. They were called BB guns. One woman had her eye put out. The CC paid for its replacement.

Oh, the fun we had! We pitched tents and roasted marshmallows and danced naked around our bonfires and drank and smoked and fucked ourselves silly. We had a wilderness experience that other folks paid a lot of money for. It was all in aid of group bonding. It was nothing like boot camp in the old movies. I sometimes wonder if having a drill instructor shout that he was going to tear off our heads and shit down our necks would have made any difference to how we fought when we finally went in against the "enemy." I doubted it.

After those maneuvers and other exercises at least as pointless, we were finally given real guns, hand weapons of a sort that had not been issued for field use in the previous thirty years or so.

I proved I could hit a three-foot target at twenty yards . . . every once in a while. I got a kick out of shooting the old things. But it was nothing compared to the thrill of handling and firing a portable drilling laser.

Our unit consisted of twenty cops and one sergeant. Most of the cops would be packing handguns and/or rifles. Projectile weapons. But each unit was to also have one laser, not because anyone, even the CC, ever intended to use them on people, but because they might come in handy if we had to burn through walls.

There's an expression, "cowboy up." Its original meaning may be lost in time, because it now has nothing to do with herding cattle. These days it means to gird your loins to face a challenge. But it also means to put on macho airs. To swagger, to be cool.

There is just no way to handle a portable drilling laser without feeling like a cowboy. On Earth, it would take at least two people to handle one. Even on Luna you can't give one to a small person. In our unit we drew lots and I was the winner. Or loser, depending on how you look at it in hindsight.

While I handled it, I was the center of attention. With the delimiter turned off, that fucker would burn a hole through six inches of steel in less than a second. It would also burn holes in rock, which is what I did.

There must be some destructive impulse in the human genes that makes many of us delight in blowing stuff up. Shooting a laser was a lot easier than a gun. You could see where the beam was going. You had a low-power aiming laser to zero in on your target, then you pulled the trigger. And *kerblooey*! Vaporized! I defy you not to get a kick out of that. My heart leaped every time one of the rocks was turned into a spray of red-hot gravel.

But soon enough we were summoned and told we were going into action. And off we marched, into the maw of the beast.

twelve _____

SHERLOCK

t is me, Sherlock.

There is something wrong with αChris.

It has been one two three days since we visited the Lucky Loonie Double-Happiness No-MSG Garden. Pumpkin told him something there, but I did not know what it was. At first it seemed like he was eager to get on the trail, and I was looking forward to tracking down Mary Smith. But then his mood changed. I could smell it all over him. He sat in front of the deep screen and watched old flat movies all day and into the night. There was one movie he watched three times in three days. It was a movie called *Chinatown*. He would drink some bourbon poison and mutter to himself.

"Forget it, Chris. It's Irontown."

I do not know what that means.

αChris does not eat much. Even worse, three times he has forgotten to feed me. I had to pick up my bowl and take it to him.

It has been two days since he gave me a Bowser Bow-wow's Bacon-flavored Doggie Snack.

I am worried. I am so worried that I did not eat all of my food last night. It is still there in the bowl. It is Lunapurina Ground Pig. Lunapurina Ground Pig is one of my favorites. But not today. It does not even smell very good. It smells like sadness. And my tummy hurts.

I will be extracautious in the next few days. For some reason I cannot explain, I am worried that αChris might hurt himself.

I would do anything to keep a human or a dog or a brontosaurus or a damn cat from harming αChris.

But how can I protect αChris from αChris?

I must think about this some more.

CHRIS

Shortly after our visit to the Chinese restaurant, I found myself with a bad case of the Big Glitch blues.

There are meds you can take for that. I tried several of them in the past. They turned me into a happy idiot with no drive to do anything more challenging than chasing butterflies in an insect park.

The blues can sometimes hit me so hard, though, that I seriously consider taking one of them again. There are worse things than chasing butterflies.

After all, I don't need the money, what little money I get from working as a freelance private detective. My settlement from the government that fucked me over so badly is enough to make me a moderately rich guy. With my current lifestyle I haven't even been able to spend all the interest.

So there's no need for me to slouch around in a battered trench coat and fedora hat with the brim turned down, pretending that what I'm doing matters to anyone other than the low-life losers who are my client base.

And that thought, of course, just made the depression worse.

Beside the chair there was the remains of four blue plate specials brought up from below. It had been an effort to rise and walk to the door to get them. My third bottle of ersatz bourbon was empty, and I didn't have the energy to call up and have another delivered.

I noticed that Sherlock had not even bothered to lick the blue plate specials clean. This disturbed me. Sherlock is never depressed, and he always licks the plates. Was he sick?

"Should we take you to the vet, old friend?" I asked him. He rested his chin on my knee and stared up at me. I saw accusation in those intelligent brown eyes.

I looked away and back to the movie I had been watching. "Forget it, Sherlock," I said, solemnly. "It's Irontown."

I closed my eyes, wishing myself back to 1930s Los Angeles, where the sky was big and the gravity was strong and the women all wore a lot of lipstick and terrific hats with wispy net veils.

What I got instead was one more descent into Hell. Memories of Irontown rose up from the gates of Hell and surrounded me.

————

There is a sculpture by Auguste Rodin that is actually called *The Gates of Hell.* You can call up a holo of it. There are 180 figures, including some that Rodin cast separately and are well-known on their own, including *The Thinker, The Kiss,* and *Eternal Springtime.* I have spent many hours staring at the repro in the museum.

There is another depiction of Hell that I'm aware of. It is in a triptych by the Dutch painter Hieronymous Bosch, called *The Garden of Earthly Delights.*

On the left side of the thing is Adam and Eve getting married.

The middle part, the largest part, is the garden the artist was talking about when he named the piece. Both panels contain images that are deeply disturbing.

But the ugliest stuff by far is in the right panel, which is clearly Hell. It is so twisted that I just can't look at it for too long. And sometimes when I do I have nightmares.

The gates to my own Hell were not nearly so dramatic. In fact, it was impossible to know just where the city I knew ended and the city of Heinleiners began. No "Here Be Dragons" sign, no "Abandon All Hope" or "Your Remains Will NOT Be Sent to Your Next of Kin."

When our raid began we were marched down a wide corridor that gradually got dimmer and dingier. We saw a few people, but they quickly scuttled out of our way. We were up close to the surface. We had been told that and very little else.

My universal positioning system was haywire. It was flashing a big UNKNOWN in my eye. Since we were off the map, I wondered how the CC knew where to send us. But I marched on.

Finally we came to a wall. It was a most unusual wall. It was a mirror surface, about ten feet square, and it completely blocked our way.

There were two sergeants at the head of our unit now. Call them Sergeant Ugly and Sergeant Uglier. I think Uglier was female.

They seemed momentarily stumped by the wall. They muttered back and forth, staying out of earshot of the troops. But something they heard over their radios seemed to reassure them. Ugly turned to us.

"Listen up, you maggots," he bellowed. Maggots? That was a new one. He had called us idiots, incompetent idiots, disgusting idiots, and stupid fuckers, but this was a new low.

"In about one minute, that wall will open up," Ugly was

saying. "Headquarters says we won't be encountering any resistance to speak of." He scoffed. "I've heard that one before, when my company was storming the dug-in Free-Belt resistance fighters on Nessus. They were practically starved out already, according to the brass hats who set it all up. And we spent the next six months digging them out one at a time.

"Is that gonna happen here? Nah, I don't see it. But I want y'all to be ready for anything, understand?"

Nessus? I had to think a moment. My solography is about average. I can name the planets and major moons and twenty or so of the minor planets, and maybe a dozen of Jupiter's moons, but after that things get a little hazy. Here on nice, cozy Luna we don't spend a lot of time thinking of the actual complexity of the Sol system, the constantly changing dance of the rocks and ice that orbit our sun. But they're out there, and many of them are inhabited. So we have comets, asteroids, trojans, TNOs, cubewanos, plutinos, sednoids, and kuiperiods. Some of those classifications overlap. Some of them have things worth mining.

Nessus is a centaur. That's a type of minor planet that orbits between Jupiter and Neptune. In this case, I'd call it extremely minor, since it's only about forty miles across. Apparently a major battle was fought over it.

"So shoulder arms, you dweebs. Lay on, you stupid Macduffs, and fuck the one who first cries 'hold, enough!'"

I just had time to register that Ugly apparently had enough of an education to know a rough form of Shakespeare. And then the mirror wall vanished.

It didn't roll up or slide to the side, it didn't fall forward or backward, it didn't sink into the floor. It didn't crumple like a sheet of aluminum foil. No, it was like it had been a soap bubble that had popped, soundlessly. It wasn't until much later that I learned that, compared to that wall, a soap bubble was as thick and hard as a walnut shell.

It was my first sight of a null field. The quantum boys and girls get into heated arguments over whether the thickness of a field is comparable to the Planck length (whatever that is) or if it has no third dimension at all. The jury is still very much out.

There was a soft *whoosh*, and my ears popped. We instinctively fear that sensation. It might mean a blowout is happening. I caught my breath, and so did several of the people around me. But it turned out it was just the pressure equalizing from the two sides of the field. Of course, I didn't know at the time that the mirror surface was a field, nor that it actually ceased to exist when it was turned off. And I still don't know how the CC managed to turn it off. No one does, for sure, but the leading theory is that it was a traitor among the Heinleiners.

Ugly shouted out a command, and we surged forward.

I said earlier that there was no sign as we entered into the depths of Hell. Come to think of it, there was one. It was a tattered banner strung from one side of the widening corridor to the other. It said:

MALL CLOSING!
EVERYTHING MUST GO!
UP TO 80% OFF SELECTED ITEMS!

That's the first thing we encountered: an abandoned neighborhood mall. It was medium-sized, say two or three hundred stores. It was probably a hundred years old and showing its age. There was a thick layer of dust over everything, showing that the filtration system had gone bad a long time ago, but the air was warm and breathable. There were puddles on the floor, and the steady sound of dripping water. The only light was the legal minimum, from fixtures high in the ceiling. Down below, everything was in perpetual gloom.

We glimpsed our first Heinleiners. What we mostly saw was their retreating backs.

They kept us moving, at a jog-trot. We quickstepped through two more malls like that one, gradually seeing some signs of human occupation, but only the fleeing backs of the humans. Then the last corridor opened out into a large space. What used to be called a megamall, before habitats many miles long and deep like the one I lived in were built. The funny thing is, this space felt bigger, probably because my brain can't really comprehend just how big the city is. But here, the space was of a size that hovered somewhere between enormous and gargantuan.

At first I couldn't make much sense of it. We are used to a certain order in our habitats. They are planned, laid out logically, according to certain zoning regulations. You can't open a hot-dog stand in a residential neighborhood, for instance. When you do find a place where you can open your stand, you need permits. You have to allow visits from the health inspector. You need to pay your business air tax.

I've never felt that our society is too regimented, too regulated, but I know some do. And the champion malcontents were now all around us.

My mind gradually put together what I was seeing. Big parts of the space were filled with large shipping containers, both the rectangular and the cylindrical kind. They were stacked as if put together by a demented child with a twisted set of Lego bricks. The ends of some of them hung out beyond the main stack and had windows and doors cut into them and stairs or ladders or just knotted ropes hanging from them.

I realized these were homes. People were living in these discarded box-cars.

Some of them were painted in a wild assortment of colors, either abstract patterns or murals. I saw one mural that might have been done by a not-too-talented kindergartner, and another that most citizens would be proud to have adorning a public building. A third showed very explicit sexual acts. I assumed that one was the residence of a sex worker.

Below many of the windows were window boxes burst-

ing with flowers or vegetables, each with a growlight sus-
pended over it. In the distance I could see what looked like
about an acre of caramel-corn growing. Right in the center
of town. No zoning laws at all.

One occupant had actually strung a line between his
window and another box across the way, and laundry was
hanging from it. It reminded me of black-and-white photos
of tenement neighborhoods in Old New York.

The first impression was definitely of a slum. But in the
few moments I had before the fan hit the shit, I revised that.
It actually looked pretty nice. There were shops all around
the periphery, selling just about anything you could want.
There were little cubbyhole restaurants. There were food
trucks, including one selling hot dogs! It was the fact that
it was all so jumbled up that threw me. After the carefully
planned cities I had known all my life, this anarchy took
some getting used to.

The place smelled good, and I realized I was pretty hungry. Not far from me was a place called Aunt Hazel's Ice
Cream Emporium and While-U-Wait Surgery Shoppe. After we had wrapped all this up, I figured I'd have a triple
scoop of something.

Sitting at a table outside Aunt Hazel's were a man and a
pregnant woman. Sitting at the woman's feet was a dog
with a jaw so massive you wondered how he could open it.

It was an English bulldog and his name was Winston.

The woman was Hildy Johnson, ace reporter for the
News Nipple.

Something raced by me, something small and pretty fast. I thought it was a dog at first, but it wasn't. It was a horse, no more than six inches high. I didn't know they made them that small. In fact, they don't, except in Heinlein Town. The horselet was a product of the illegal gene tinkering we were supposedly there to stop.

I heard the voice of a sergeant—not one of ours—who called out from the far side of the mall.

"Everybody freeze, and nobody will get hurt."

I hefted my laser, wishing I hadn't won the lottery to get the privilege of carrying it. I'd have preferred just a handgun . . .

. . . just like the ones that I noticed the three civilians closest to me were packing, in holsters on their belts. Hey, nobody told us . . .

It looked like we had at least achieved the element of surprise. None of the armed people I could see drew down on us. Which, of course, was the smart thing to do when confronted with a few hundred people dressed in combat gear, all with guns leveled at you.

My fellow invaders moved forward smartly, relieving the stunned citizens of their weaponry. For those first few minutes it seemed like things were going okay.

Over at the ice cream parlor, I saw that some sort of ruckus was happening. One of us, a regular cop and her sergeant, didn't seem to be working on the same team. The sergeant started toward Hildy Johnson, and the man she was with—a teenager, I now saw—moved between them. Without breaking stride the sergeant swung his rifle butt against the kid's jaw. I could hear it crack from a hundred feet away.

That wasn't what it was supposed to be at all. I didn't think I could do anything about it at the moment, but I intended to get the big ape's name and serial number and report him to the police board.

The woman cop seemed to agree with me. She had words with the sergeant, but ended up snapping one end of a pair of handcuffs over Johnson's wrist. That was when Johnson decided to resist. She pulled away, but this woman knew how to subdue a rowdy. She twisted Johnson's arm and bent her over the table where she had been sitting. Johnson ended up with her face in the remains of an ice-cream sundae.

Suddenly the bulldog came up from under the table, flying through the air like a squat rocket, and clamped those incredible jaws onto the policewoman's arm. She screamed as loudly as I've ever heard anyone scream. The sergeant had turned away to deal with something else. Now he turned again and came at the woman and the bulldog with his sidearm drawn. I figured the dog had breathed his last.

That's when the sergeant's chest exploded.

Something powerful enough to pierce his armor had blown through his chest. There was another shot through the chest, then most of his head disappeared in a shower of metallic skull, brains, and the red mist of blood.

I'm not ashamed to say that my first reaction was to throw myself to the ground and look for something to crawl under. Others around me, both cops and local citizens, were doing the same thing. There was nothing close, so I scrambled on hands and knees across the floor, feeling as if my own spine would be severed by a bullet any moment.

I don't think it was more than a few seconds until I reached a big concrete planter with a palm tree growing in it. Looking back at where I had been, I was amazed at how far I'd come. If they held Olympic crawling races, I figure I would have earned the gold.

I wanted to keep my head down more than anything, but it seemed wiser to keep abreast of developing threats, so I risked popping up a few times. I saw people sprinting across the open mall, but every time I looked, there were fewer and fewer of them as they found places to shelter. I could see dozens, then hundreds more sergeants and bobbies pouring in from all sides of the mall. Our contingent hadn't been the only group, and I knew there were others who would be following behind my company. The idea had been to flood the place with overwhelming force, run everybody in, book them, then sort it all out. It should have worked, and with any other group of people, I'm sure it would have.

I heard bullets hitting all over the place. Then I saw a bobby go down, shot through the shoulder. He screamed in pain, then either died or passed out. I never found out which. We lost eighty-six bobbies that day, and he could very well have been one of them.

Most of the gunfire seemed to be coming from up high. People were turning their homes into sniper's nests. I saw at least three of them, and there were probably more.

I barely had time to register that when Uglier went down, missing most of her left leg. She was clearly made of sterner stuff than the wounded bobby, or me for that matter. She never made a sound but spun around as she fell and sprayed bullets in the direction the shot had come from. Then she dragged herself to shelter behind an overturned table and proceeded to calmly pull a tourniquet tight around the stump of her leg. I mean, sure, it would be replaced if she lived, but how does someone endure that level of pain and still operate?

I had never felt all that much camaraderie with any of the sergeants, but dammit, she was in my unit, and I figured I ought to try and do something about it.

I looked around, then up, and saw someone high in the stacked maze, leaning out a window and aiming a large rifle downward. It looked to be about where the shot had come from.

My drilling laser was on the ground a few feet away from me. I didn't remember dropping it. To get it back, I would have to expose myself, or part of myself, anyway. I looked around the windows above me and didn't see anyone, and stuck my right foot out. I managed to hook my bootheel over the strap and, after losing it twice, pulled it back behind the planter with me. I popped my head up again and looked around quickly.

Others were pouring bullets into a window on the fifth or sixth level of the maze, shattering the hard plastic wall.

I guessed that's where most of the shots had been coming from, and leveled my laser at it and hit the firing button.

The green beam of light sliced through the gun smoke and kept right on slicing, through the plastic and right into the walls beyond. Something inside exploded, and bright orange flames erupted from the remains of the window.

I didn't like that much. The damn laser was not the right weapon for this fight. It was way too powerful. I had assumed it was mostly there as a show of strength, and as I said before, I had never expected to use it.

There was no way of telling just how far that damn thing had penetrated, or if any innocent civilians had been in the way. I didn't like the idea that I might have killed someone who had nothing to do with this fight . . . but I will admit that I was a lot less concerned about the possibility than I had been ten minutes ago. Combat does that to you.

Ten minutes? Is that all the time it had been? I checked my time display and, close enough, it had been only eleven. At that point, I had just five minutes more to go in what I've come to think of as my first life.

thirteen _____

"You be a good dog while I'm away," I said to Sherlock. I scratched behind his ears, and he let his tongue hang out as he enjoyed it. I briefly wished I could be as carefree and content with life as a dog. Sherlock was a special dog, a supersmart dog, but in the end he was a dog, after all. How worried could he be about a trip to the outskirts of Irontown?

"You stay here and hold down the fort, old friend." He looked up adoringly at me. I know he understood that I had told him to stay and to guard the place, as if it needed guarding.

I arranged with downstairs to bring him food if I was away longer than I intended. I didn't really like leaving Sherlock behind, but I felt this trip might be dangerous, it might be confrontational, and I didn't know for sure how he might react if he saw me threatened. I couldn't have him biting people. Maybe I was doing him an injustice, but I wanted to err on the side of caution.

Besides, between what Mom had told me and what I had learned from the girl who called herself Pumpkin, I at last had something to go on. It was a long way from what you might call solid, but it was something.

———————

But a bit before that . . .

When I returned to the restaurant, I asked the owner if I could talk to Pumpkin for a while. He was reluctant but became a lot more cooperative when I slipped him a sawbuck.

"You get ten minutes," he said.

Sherlock followed me into the kitchen.

I could tell at once that Pumpkin was not the spiciest pepper in the hot and sour soup. She was the owner's daughter and had worked there as long as she could remember. She did all sorts of work in the kitchen that could have easily been done by robots, and she was proud of this. I would never have told her it was because she was cheaper, in the end, than a machine. She was happy in her work. If she liked to spend her days cutting up celery and washing woks, that was fine with me.

I learned most of this in the first few minutes of my questioning, and none of it was the result of questions. She was one of those persons who chatters incessantly, and once she got started, it was hard to steer her in the direction you wanted her to go. She liked to talk about herself, and I got an earful of her pretty boring life story.

Like any cop, I can listen to someone I'm interrogating for a long time, knowing that people often say a lot more than they intend to. With Pumpkin, that would not be a problem. There was nothing in her life she felt like she needed to hide. She had no deep, dark secrets.

Sherlock was curled up under a prep table chasing dream rabbits by the time I nudged her in the direction of Mary Smith. I showed her my composite picture, and she brightened at once.

"Oh, yes, Delphine! Our new cook! She is my friend for months and months."

"Just months?"

"Oh, yes! Baba hired her months ago. She is a very good cook. Her moo shu bronto is much better than the old cook made. Also her twice-cooked lizard with garlic sauce. And her—"

"Do you know where she lives?"

"And it's a funny thing. She came through the air grate just like you did. I was scared! She told me not to tell anyone about . . ."

Her hand flew to her mouth. I had the feeling she had never been able to keep a secret in her whole life.

"Oh, I did it again. Pumpkin, why can't you keep your mouth shut?" She actually smacked herself on the cheek and looked very sad.

"It's okay," I told her. "I have something to give her. She won't mind that you let it slip."

Pumpkin brightened at once. I doubted she could remain worried about anything for very long unless it was right there in front of her.

"Do you know where she lives?" I asked again. "Do you know her whole name?"

She made a gesture twirling her finger around the side of her head, which I took to mean something like, "Information flies in one ear and out the other." But she took me to a terminal and looked up her employment application.

Delphine RR Blue Suede Shoes. Oh, terrific. A Presley-ite *and* a Westerosian, with para-leprosy.

There was an address. It was not actually in Irontown—there are no real addresses in Irontown, you have to know somebody who can tell you how to get there—but it was within walking distance.

"What do you think, Sherlock?" I asked him. "You think we'll find her there?"

The dog sprang to his feet and looked up at me with his tongue hanging out. Sherlock knows many, many words, but there are a handful that he likes more than others. *Find* is one of them. He was all set to get on her trail. If only I had a piece of her clothing to give him.

———

But I decided I'd better leave Sherlock behind. I knew where I was going.

Ms. Blue Suede Shoes's neighborhood was overdue for some urban renewal. It was reachable only on a train that clattered a bit as it wobbled down the rails, one of a series of small malls strung out along the rail tunnel like . . . well, pearls is not a good analogy, unless it was the ones that were cast before swine.

These were the abodes of people with absolutely no marketable skills that could lead to a job, or no inclination to get a job. Society guaranteed them air, housing, water, and food.

But the air didn't have to be odor-free.

The housing needn't be more than a cubicle with a spigot for metallic-tasting water (shower and toilet down the hall, and cross your fingers that either of them worked), and a microwave.

The food was edible. That was the best that could be said for it.

As in any place where things were in short supply, there was a thriving black market in anything people might desire. The economy was largely barter, off the books.

Any cop was familiar with places like this. A high percentage of our work always took us to slums like this.

I smelled moldy socks and sweaty armpits. I wondered how often they washed or changed the air filters around here? Weekly? Yearly? Decadely? I know that's not a word, but it somehow seemed right for this neighborhood.

I found Delphine's level, then her corridor. It was narrow, as they tended to be around here. There were a couple of grubby, naked small children, maybe four or five, playing with a scruffy lion cub. There was a disassembled playbot beside them. It had not been taken apart carefully. I wondered if they planned to take the cub apart when they were through.

I stepped around them. The lion cub's hair stood on end, and she hissed at me as I passed. The children actually looked more feral than the little lion.

Ms. Shoes's apartment was at the far end of the corridor, what people referred to as the "bedrock" end, though there was not much chance it was actually up against the Lunar bedrock. If you went through the fire-escape door at the end, you would almost certainly find yourself in a stairwell, with another door on the other side of the landing that led to the end of another corridor.

The door leading to the cubicle of Delphine RR Blue Suede Shoes was plain, and slightly battered, as if someone had tried to get in without a print. I'm sure he left in frustration.

Beside the door was a large canvas bag, an old-fashioned duffel with a drawstring pulled tight.

I pressed the plate and faintly heard, "Well it's one for the money, two for the show, three to get ready now go cat go!"

"Well, it could have been worse," I muttered. "It could have been 'Hound Dog.'" Anyone alive in Luna is familiar with at least half a dozen Elvis songs because the Church of Celebrity Saints makes sure you encounter at least one every day.

In one of my old detective books and movies, the shamus would take a step back and kick the door open with his black-leather wingtip. If he tried that on a Lunar door, he could break his ankle. Even an abode as humble as this one would have a pressure door that sealed tighter than a constipated frog's ass, as Mom used to say during breeding season.

If the door looked really sturdy, a fictional detective would get out his trusty picklock. Even if this door had a pickable mechanical lock—which it did not—I wouldn't know how to pick it.

But one legacy from my time as a cop was knowing how to bypass a touchplate even if you don't have the right fingerprint. It's known as a Universal Passcode Unit. Cops call them jimmies and can check them out when serving a warrant. They are supposed to be returned to the property master after they've been used, but they are one of those items that somehow keep going missing. Most cops can figure out a way to take one home and never return it. I had done so, and I still had it.

I held the UPU against the touchplate and let it do its thing.

It was taking long enough that I began to get nervous. No matter that they are called universal, jimmies are *not* capable of picking the highest-security locks. There are systems that will alert the local precinct if someone attempts an unauthorized entry. Very few private residences have them, and it didn't seem likely that there would be one here in the suburbs of Irontown, but I couldn't be sure. Sometimes people engaged in illegal activity have their own systems, and they don't report to the police. They send out a silent signal to some very large and very nasty folks who specialize in knocking heads together. Or removing them. Painfully.

I was about to beat it down the hallway when there was a click and the door opened inward a few inches. I pushed it open slowly.

I pushed the door open all the way. The light came on automatically, a very dim overhead panel.

The room was all but empty.

Lying on the floor, up against the far wall—all of eight feet away from me—was a slab of foam of the type you would find if you removed the ticking from a mattress. Lying on top of it was a pillow and a neatly folded blanket. There was a single folding chair.

That was it for furniture. In one corner was a sink. A mirror was on the wall behind it. There was a built-in table against another wall, with connections for power and cyber access.

Ah, well. I got the duffel bag from the hall and dumped its contents on the table. I sat down on the chair and started going through it.

It didn't take long. There were a dozen plastic food trays

from various restaurants that delivered. I learned that she had a weakness for Chinese, which would make sense, given the last job she had worked. For variety she occasionally had a box from the neighborhood taco shop. Every once in a while, donuts for dessert.

Before going through it all, I looked all around the place again. I tried to imagine living there. I tried to imagine what a sad existence it must be. Or must have been, since all the signs were that she had moved out. Sitting in the chair, eating chow mein with a plastic fork. Thinking about getting out and dancing with dubious partners at a sleazy nightclub, coming home with a case of resistant leprosy . . .

It was surely possible that she had had more personal items, more furniture, maybe a touch of decoration . . . but somehow it didn't feel like that. To me, it felt like a hideout. It felt like she had gone to ground here. I might have been reading too much into my single meeting with her, but she just didn't seem like someone who had grown up in a pit like this.

And there was also the matter of her job. She hadn't had it long, but I knew she must have made a salary that could have easily paid for a much nicer place in a much nicer neighborhood.

So what was she doing here?

I sighed and turned back to the discarded stuff.

There was a green tunic with the name "Delphine RR" printed under the words "No-MSG Garden," and a high chef's hat. I wondered briefly why chefs would wear such a ridiculous lid, but I guess a guy sporting a twentieth-century fedora shouldn't toss stones.

There was a white apron with brown stains on it that I assumed were the remains of food.

The only vaguely personal item was a wilted bunch of yellow daisies and a cracked ceramic vase with a geometric pattern in red and black.

What was *not* there? For one thing, there was no matchbook with "The Frolic Room" printed on it, like Philip Marlowe might have found in Los Angeles. There was no handkerchief with the initials of the murderer embroidered on it, smelling of chloroform, as Miss Marple might have found in the drawing-room wastebasket.

In short, I didn't see anything that a detective-story writer would have invented to guide my next steps in the pursuit of my missing client.

Which meant I would now have to look up either the address Hopper had given me a few days ago in the Nighthawk or somehow try to make a connection with the ancient Mr. Scrooge.

Which meant a trip deep into Irontown.

I shuddered and turned to go, then realized I was missing something. In the stories, when they speak of thoroughly searching a place, the mystery writers said the hero or the cops *tossed* it. There was almost nothing to toss in the sad little cubicle.

Just the mattress. If it had been an old-fashioned spring construction like in the movies, I would have cut it open.

People apparently liked to hide stuff in there. Since pretty much all mattresses these days were slabs of foam like this one—or thinner, since with Lunar gravity it was possible to be fairly comfortable on a bed of nails—there was nothing to be done there. But the other place people liked to hide stuff was *under* the mattress. Misers kept their money there, or so it was said.

So I lifted it.

There was a pair of gloves. I felt sure they were the ones she had worn in my office. There was her crazy hat with the peacock feathers, crushed almost flat. And there was a piece of paper. I picked it up. I read it. It was in a lovely cursive hand:

Sorry about this, Mr. Bach.

I heard something behind me and turned in time to see the pressure door close. The next sound I heard was the distinctive *chunk* of the wards sliding home. Every Lunarian knows that sound from his first pressure drill as a toddler.

"Hey!" I shouted. I pounded on the door.

That's when I heard the hiss of gas coming from the air duct high in the wall. The gas had a greenish tint to it.

I held my breath, but you can only do that for so long. I felt consciousness slipping away.

The last thing I thought I heard was the sound of barking.

fourteen _____

At the beginning of the Irontown raid, I did not know the pregnant woman I saw at the ice-cream parlor was Hildy Johnson, the reporter who later wrote a best-selling account of the Big Glitch. It was only later, reading her book, that I was shocked to see that I had been a part of her story. Our paths crossed for only seconds, and I doubt she remembers much about me at all. But there is no way I will ever forget it.

———————

I understand it is common to lose memory of events leading up to a terrible event. In my case I didn't lose much, but the memories are all filed at random. It's as if the various scenes were printed out on cards, which were then tossed in the air, picked up, and stacked by a chimp. Every time I try to think of it (which is as seldom as possible) things seem to be happening in a different sequence.

I see myself firing while the reporter and her friend are spooning up their hot fudge or pistachio, or whatever, and at the same time I see Winston, the mutt, taking a big chunk out of the female cop's leg.

For a time after firing into the apartment with my laser, I just concentrated on keeping my head down. I cursed the goddamn sergeants, Ugly and Uglier and Ugliest and Even Uglier Than That and *Unbelievably* Ugly, for not providing me with a projectile weapon, like most of the rest of the company had. I felt naked, exposed, with nothing to fight back with if someone came at me with deadly intent, except something that could ignite half the mall.

I almost left the laser behind when I made my break for better shelter. If I had, things would have been very different.

We can all point into our pasts and find moments like that, to be sure, but there are not many that are so clearly life-changing.

What I had chosen was a space beneath a steel structure off to one side of the open area. There was no one else there, and it looked solid enough to stop most bullets. It was a platform with thirteen steps leading up to it. There was no railing up there, just a steel framework: two upright I-beams and another beam spanning between them.

This was the Irontown gallows. Heinleiners believed in capital punishment and also felt strongly that if someone really needed killing by the community, it should be done in full view of that community, not hidden away in a prison.

If I had known it was a gallows, would I have chosen it as a place to hide? Damn straight I would. It looked like the most solid structure I could reach without a long, long run. I'm not superstitious.

So I crossed my fingers, spit on the ground, recited the few words of the Hail Mary that I could remember from films, and started running.

I hadn't gone more than five long steps before a bullet hit me in the vest. It was bullet-resistant, but trust me, it's not something you want to experience. It stopped me in my tracks, and I fell backward. I could literally hear two more bullets pass above me.

So I crawled.

I could hear firing, but I didn't want to raise my head to see where it was coming from. Trust me again, in a situation like that you want to make yourself as small as possible.

But it was taking too long. I decided getting to cover was more important than staying low. The longer I was out there, the better chance someone would notice me crawling. I would have to rely on the vest to stop the flying metal. Aware all the time, of course, that my head was not the least bit bulletproof.

Two more bullets hit me almost at once, but I managed to stay on my feet and stagger forward.

I don't know at what point I was hit in the arm. I don't recall feeling it. I think I didn't even know I had been hit until I crouched under the gallows. Then I felt warm liquid flowing down my right bicep, looked down, saw the bullet hole in my tunic, and almost passed out.

But I stuck a finger in the hole in the cloth and tore it open. I saw it was more of a graze than a through-and-through, though there was a small, blackened flap of flesh dangling from the wound. It wasn't bleeding too badly. No need for a tourniquet.

For a while it didn't even hurt. Then all at once it burned like fire.

———————

Here is where my recollections and the story told by Hildy Johnson part company. Now, I'm not about to call her a liar. She has stated that she changed certain details in her account to protect people who did not wish their names to be used. It may well be that she also altered some events for reasons of her own, again possibly having to do with secrets of the Heinleiners they do not wish to have exposed.

All I know for sure is that things could *not* have happened as she described them, or I would not be here to tell about it. So I was briefly a character in her story, and she was a character in mine. She would continue to be one for just a little while longer, and we would part never having known who the other was.

Not only was the platform of the gallows a nice grade of steel, someone had stowed some crates beneath it. They were not steel, just high-grade packing plastic, and I had no idea what was in them, but whatever it was, it seemed to be enough. I heard bullets *whang* off the gallows above me, and heard the softer *whump* when something hit one of the crates, but nothing was coming through. I was prepared to sit there barricaded behind a crate listening to *whangs* and *whumps* until the sun burned out, if need be. I couldn't imagine what would bring me out into the open again.

Then she stumbled into my view, all four-foot-six and seventy pounds of her, looking totally lost and utterly terrified.

I guessed she was about ten. She had rather tangled long blond hair and wore the sort of blue jumpsuit common among the Heinleiners who had null-field suits implanted in their bodies. She seemed disoriented, stumbling around the field of fire like a zombie.

No one really knows just how much starch they have in them until they are faced with a situation where something dangerous must be done. That's when you find out; you really can't know until that moment.

Will you run, or will you go in harm's way?

I'll tell you this. I really wanted to run. I admit it. But I was still a cop. One definition of a cop is that he or she is the person who, when there is gunfire or an explosion, runs *toward* the disturbance, not away. If I stayed there, I'd no longer be able to think of myself as a cop. Or as a worthwhile human being, for that matter.

I didn't think about it for more than a couple of seconds. I shoved one of the crates aside and sprinted toward the lost little girl.

It was at least partly luck. For a few seconds, the sounds of the fight were not so loud, the sound of bullets flying by not so frequent.

That's when I really tried to ditch the laser. It was too bulky and heavy to be carrying around, especially if I didn't intend to use it. That's when I found out it had snagged on my vest. There it was, flopping around, getting in my way, and I just didn't have the time to find out which of the many attachments of my combat uniform it had hung up on. Cursing, I got hold of it with my weakened right hand.

I was thumping along as gracefully as any three-legged camel. I was a few feet away from her when a spray of bullets landed all around her, *spanging* off the concrete floor. Until that moment, I would have told you that the old standby scene in action movies—you know the one, where Our Hero is bracketed by little explosive squibs that are meant to represent bullets but remains unharmed— was flatly impossible. Yet at least twenty bullets impacted before her, behind her, to each side of her, and possibly even went between her legs . . . and not a one of them hit her.

If we survived this, I thought, I'm taking her to the racetrack. She had to be the luckiest person who ever lived.

Not totally lucky, though. Though all the flying metal missed her, most of them left their mark on the concrete floor. And though this never happens in action movies, hundreds of particles of concrete grit, large and small, flew up into the air.

The smaller ones were stopped by her coverall, but she was hit by a dozen of the larger ones. None of them were big enough to make a terrible wound, but they certainly stung like hell, and she yipped and jumped into the air. I could see little spots of blood blooming on her legs and arms and one on her forehead.

She yipped even louder when I tackled her. She started hitting me with her little fists. I yelled that I was trying to *help* her, dammit, but the battle was too loud for her to hear me. Her fists were the least of my worries, anyway. The tempo of the gunfire was picking up again, and I saw at least two laser beams sizzling overhead.

I managed to keep on my feet as I executed a turn that was probably even *worse* than a three-legged camel, and headed back toward the gallows.

That's when a finger of laser light probed into the gallows and the crates underneath exploded in flames.

Some days it just doesn't pay to get out of bed, does it?

With my struggling burden under one arm and my ridiculous Flash Gordon Photonic Ray-gun hanging from my other, I turned away from the flames and looked around for other shelter.

There wasn't much. The most promising seemed to be a line of mobile food carts about a hundred feet away from us, in the direction of the ice-cream parlor, which was now in flames, too. The girl was shouting at me now.

"Put me down, you big ape!"

"Shut up, or I *will* put you down and you can look out for yourself!"

"I'll kill you, so help me, I'll kill you! What are you guys doing? Why are you killing us?"

I didn't have time to think about that then. At least she had stopped struggling.

We were blessed by another lull in the fighting, and I made it to the line of trucks. I could see bullet holes here and there, but it didn't look like there had been concentrated fire on them. Pick one, Chris. Voodoo donuts? Sergei's bronto tacos? Atomic Fission Chips?

On the side of one truck it said "The Quackin' Wok, featuring sizzling duck stir-fry!" It looked substantial, with the service door slammed down tight and the access door at the back standing open. It had the added advantage that it was the closest portable ptomaine palace to us.

I hurried to the door and tossed the girl inside before

I had had a chance to look in there myself. It wasn't until she screamed that I saw that the proprietor was lying on the floor in a pool of blood. A good bit of his head was missing.

It was the scream that got the attention of Hildy Johnson and her Hound from Hell.

The kid launched herself out of the wagon like her ass was on fire and collided with me. She was bloody all over. She was still screaming.

"Hey, put her down!"

The command came from behind me. I turned and faced Johnson. The bulldog was standing beside her, and he looked horrible. He was bleeding badly, and seemed dazed. Johnson was pointing a rifle at me.

The girl chose that moment to finally wriggle free. She darted off, away from us both.

"And drop that weapon," Johnson added.

"You put your gun down," I said.

"What the hell is that? A laser?"

"Put your gun down," I repeated. "You're under arrest."

"What are you, a cop?"

"That's right," I said. "Put that rifle down, or I'll shoot." I had no intention of shooting even though the Uglies had told us that if someone pointed a gun at us, it would be stupid to wait for them to fire the first shot. I could see the logic in that. But I was carrying a drilling laser.

And here once again our stories don't exactly jibe. This is where my blurry recollections become positively chaotic.

But in the next second or two these things happened, though not necessarily in this order:

Winston the bulldog came flying up from the floor, headed right for my leg. It was an image right out of a horror movie.

I took a step back.

I pointed my laser at Winston. Johnson says I pointed it at her.

I heard the click of the trigger as Johnson fired her rifle. How I heard it over the din of battle I can't explain, but I'm sure I heard it.

The rifle didn't fire. The ammunition clip was empty.

My finger twitched on the laser's trigger. Maybe it was a voluntary twitch, maybe it was a reflex twitch. For whatever reason, my finger twitched.

The laser fired.

My world exploded.

———————

Here's what happened:

Hildy Johnson had recently had a nullsuit installed. No one outside of Irontown had ever seen or heard of this device. You still can't get one, even if you are a multibillionaire. They are not for sale.

What happens is, instantaneously a null field forms around your body. You become like one of those silver statues on top of baseball or tennis trophies, though without the bat or racket.

This second skin is perfectly reflective, and impermeable. It can be switched on manually, or it can turn itself on when it senses that its user is in a vacuum. Suddenly, it is a perfect space suit, though with a limited supply of oxygen. I don't know how much, though I know it's less than a regular space suit's air supply.

It also turns on automatically if something . . . say, a high-velocity bullet . . . intrudes into the field. In that case, the field freezes temporarily. All that kinetic energy has to go somewhere, and it seems that it bleeds off on both sides of the field. Which means that the person inside the null-suit can get uncomfortably hot. In fact, if the suit is hit by sustained gunfire, the person inside can pretty much par boil. That happened to a few Heinleiners during the pitched battle.

But that doesn't concern me here. What is a problem is that one of the things the suit field will stop is high-powered lasers.

The worst thing you can do with a powerful laser is to fire it at a mirror. And if I had shot mine at a flat mirror, I wouldn't be here to tell you this story. They would still be picking blackened bits of me out of the pavement of Irontown. But the mirror my beam hit was one that perfectly followed the bumps and hollows of Hildy Johnson's body. The beam reflected all over the place. That meant it was weakened some.

But being weakened *some* was not enough. Not nearly enough.

———————

Once more, words just don't seem adequate to describe the confusion of the moments immediately following.

I don't remember falling down. I remember lying there, looking up at the ceiling. I smelled something burning. It was me.

I tried to lift myself up but only one arm was working at all, and that one wasn't doing too well. But I got my head up and looked down at myself.

When I say I was on fire I don't mean that my clothes were just smoldering. There were flames erupting from at least three areas on my body.

There was a long furrow gashed obliquely across both of my legs. I could easily have bled to death from either leg, but the burning beam had cauterized the wounds. There was no blood spurting. There was another black gash across my belly. The clothes around that area were burning, too. The third wound was across my left arm. More flames, and this time a little blood was flowing. I managed to shift myself a bit, and noticed with a strange, calm detachment that most of that arm didn't move with me. It was entirely severed just below the elbow.

It didn't even hurt very badly. At first.

The real fun came later. Then there are no words to describe the pain. That was still down the road a bit, but not all that far away.

I managed to roll over on my side, on the left side where

the severed arm was still attached by some threads of my clothes. That smothered some of the fire. I slapped at the fire on my belly. I suppose I was actually fanning the flames without meaning to. But I didn't know what else to do, so I kept trying to beat them out with my one good arm.

There came a point where I simply gave up and waited to die.

But I didn't die.

Still burning, I looked over to the general area where Johnson had been. She wasn't there, but her dog was. He had been finished off by my laser bouncing off Johnson. It was probably for the best.

I was finally able, mercifully, to pass out. But it didn't last for long, and when I came to again the flames were still burning. I think that's when I began screaming.

Suddenly I was inundated in ice cream.

Actually it was mostly cold water and ice, but there were chunks of dark brown chocolate and red strawberry mixed in with it. Oh, good. Someone had decided that what I needed most was a Neapolitan sundae.

I sputtered. Even in your death throes, I discovered, having a bucket of ice water splashed in your face was a bit of a shock. I looked up and saw that the person who had doused me was the girl I had tried to pull out of the line of fire.

I might as well tell something I learned only later. Her name was Gretel. I will also admit that Gretel is not her real name. I know what her real name is, but just as Hildy Johnson did in her account, I'll use pseudonyms when referring to Irontown residents.

"Oh, man, you are hurt *bad*," she breathed, leaning over and looking at me. She was amazingly calm, considering that the battle was still raging. Her jumpsuit had scorch marks on it where it had been set afire, but her nullsuit seemed to have protected her from major harm.

"Get away," I choked out. "You're going to get killed."

"Shut up," she said, not unkindly. Then she grabbed the back of my collar and started to drag me. I passed out.

It was pain that brought me around again.

The first thing I noticed was that my arm was gone. The strip of cloth that had kept it attached had torn completely while she was dragging me. Well, I'd just have to buy a new one. It was the least of my worries. The arm stump didn't hurt much, but the rest . . . it was getting worse by the minute.

I must have groaned.

"Hush!" Gretel hissed. "There's a group of cops coming this way."

She had dragged me into a recessed cubbyhole of some kind. We were not perfectly concealed, but it was tons better than where I had been.

I couldn't see much at all except her face from below. I saw her tense, then relax slightly. There was a loud explosion. I heard a whistling sound. That sound, and all other sounds, quickly diminished. There was a sharp pain in my ears. Air rushed out of my lungs.

I looked up and saw that Gretel had become a silver trophy figure. The mirror face moved, looking down at me.

There had been a blowout. We were in vacuum.

At that moment, I accepted that I was about to die. Oddly enough, I wasn't too bothered about it all, except for the awful feeling of not being able to catch my breath.

At least it would stop hurting, I figured.

B ut Gretel wasn't having it.

There are stories of people surviving for unlikely periods of time in a vacuum. Five minutes? So it has been claimed. But no one has ever documented such a thing. The general opinion is that two minutes is about the limit. Some have been revived beyond that, but they were never good for much anymore, intellectually.

They say you lose consciousness in about fifteen seconds. I think I lasted a little longer than that because I remember being dragged for a moment, then lifted into the air.

Even in Lunar gravity, I was quite a burden for a small ten-year-old girl. But Gretel slung me over her shoulder like a sack of cement. Then I was bobbing up and down as she ran with me.

The last thing I remember was seeing an old familiar sign: a blue circle with the number 8 in the middle. "Oxygen Here!"

Then I was gone.

———

It seemed they had emergency pressure shelters even in Irontown. Knowing libertarian Heinleiners, all of them suspicious of most public facilities, I would expect to get a bill for using one.

When I came to again, I was lying on the floor of a six-by-six-by-six-foot cube.

Several things happen to you if you're in vacuum.

The water on your tongue begins to boil. Not because it's hot but from the zero pressure. I'm sorry to say that you shit yourself. You can't help it. It's the gas in your intestine swelling up and forcing its way out. You may also piss yourself and vomit, but I didn't do either of those.

Still, the emergency cubicle didn't smell all that great.

The pain was starting to really settle in and make itself at home. I screamed, and blood came out of my mouth. Gretel crouched over me. She was sprayed with blood but didn't really seem to notice it.

"Your lungs must be damaged," she said. She seemed almost clinically detached, but I suspected there was screaming panic just underneath. But she was consulting her internal display after googling "Extreme vacuum exposure; treatment of."

She went to one wall where there was a box with a big red cross on it. She opened it and stuff spilled out in a jumble. She crouched down and sorted through it. She came back with a pair of scissors.

"I need to cut your clothes off," she said.

"Don't," I managed to croak.

"I have to, dude. It's for the burns. We need to get some air to them.

"Please don't."

"I'll do it quickly."

The human mind is not able to retain a memory of extreme pain. You would go mad if you could actually call up that much pain or, worse, if the memory sneaked up on you. No, I remember understanding *at that moment* that I had never experienced anything like the pain I endured as she cut my clothing away. But I can't remember what it actually felt like.

See, in some places the cloth and plastic of my combat uniform had melted into my skin. They were one and the same and didn't want to part. Gretel pulled tentatively at first.

"If you're going to do it," I croaked, "then just do it!"

So she did. With the sound of tearing cloth, she ripped the awful stuff away from me. Once she turned aside and vomited, but other than that, she was a lot calmer than I would have been.

I passed out at least twice more as she worked. Each time it was a blessing. Each time I woke up again, it was a curse.

When I came to again, she was leaning over me, slapping my face.

"Wake up, man!" she said. "What the hell is your name, anyway?" I saw now that she was crying.

"Christ," I said.

"Christ? Really?"

"Chris. Christopher Bach, city police."

"I ought to just leave you alone to die, you bastard. Maybe I will."

"That would suit me fine," I said.

"After all I've gone through? No way. Now I need you to listen. Please, can you still hear me?"

I saw that she had taken off her jumper. What I could see of her was bony and blood-spattered. I wondered why she had stripped.

"There are things I need. I have to go out and get them."

"Go ahead. Get out of here."

"I'll be back, I promise. Maybe I can find some help, if you creeps haven't killed all my people." She had to stop and sob for a moment. Then she wiped tears away with the back of her hand.

"This shelter was designed to be a refuge in case of a sudden blowout. But that's all. They thought that rescue would come along in an hour or so. And maybe it will . . . but maybe it won't. I haven't been able to talk to any of my family or friends. I googled a few things when we first got here, but now I'm getting nothing. The system seems to be down. I don't know why. I'm guessing there's been a lot of damage to the net."

She almost surrendered to tears again, and I could see her pull herself together. This kid had more moxie than a battalion of Uglies.

"See, there's no air lock. I don't need one. Hell, I don't even need the shelter. What I'm going to have to do is let all the air out of here, open the door, go out, then seal it behind me. I think I can do it in about ten seconds if there's no one out there shooting at me. You should have enough oh-two pressure again in thirty seconds, tops. I just want you to be ready for it."

"Your name is Gretel?" Remember, that's not her real name.

"Yes. Now, are you ready?"

Is anyone ever ready for that? But I nodded.

"I'll knock three times on the door when I'm back and am about to open the door again. You know not to try to hold your breath?"

"Right. Open my mouth."

"You've got it. I'll try to be back soon."

"Gretel? I could sure use a drink of water."

She looked very upset.

"I'm not sure that's what you do with a burn patient. I'll have to look it up, if I can. But first I have to do this. Okay?"

"I'm very thirsty."

"Just hang on, okay? Be strong, Christopher Bach."

I nodded. I heard the air hissing out of the chamber, and what little I had in my abused lungs came rushing out, too. Instantly, her nullsuit turned on, and she became a mirror.

And it was a twisted mirror, like before, since it followed the shape of her body only a few millimeters away from her skin. But in her relatively flat chest I could see a twisted reflection of myself.

I'm sure if I had had any air in my lungs I would have screamed. What I saw reflected in her suit didn't look much like a face.

She was as good as her word, getting out the door and sealing it within ten seconds. Everything dimmed, dimmed some more . . . and then things slowly came back into focus as the chamber filled with life-giving air. When the correct pressure was reached the air spigot stopped hissing. I was left alone with my thoughts.

I never did get a real good look at the remains of my face. But I can never erase that distorted image of myself from my memory. It was an image out of a horror movie. My nose was gone. The whole left side of my face was mostly missing. In places, the bare bone of my skull was exposed. The hair was scorched off on the left side. I was badly roasted meat.

I try to imagine what someone living in, say, the twentieth century would be going through, looking at a face like that. Knowing that it wasn't going to ever get much better.

Then there is the question of pain.

I have said that the pain I suffered while in the emergency shelter was indescribable, and it was. But when I was finally taken out of the shelter and put into treatment, the pain was over. For our ancestors, the pain never stopped for the most severe cases.

For a while I thought Gretel was able to deal with the horror of my face, my burned-off arm, and my other terrible burns because, as a resident of Irontown, she sometimes came into contact with the disease and disfigurement junkies who lived there. That was not strictly true. Irontown was not a single bloc of people. In fact, many Heinleiners didn't accept that they were in Irontown at all. And they could make a pretty good case since nowhere on city maps or regional maps does a place called Irontown appear. It was the same with Heinlein Town. The fact was that Heinleiners looked on the underclass population who were their neighbors—think of it as Lower Irontown—with the same contempt that everyone else did.

A bunch of losers, Gretel said to me once when we were talking about things to try to get my mind off the pain. She had seldom seen the people who had purposely disfigured their faces into things that would make the Phantom of the Opera recoil in terror. The few times she did, she was disgusted, not scared.

All my memories from that point on are mixed together even more badly than before the battle. I never did find out what stuff she had found on the outside, nor where she found it. I knew very little about what she was doing to me, except that most of it was very painful. Oddly, though, some of it didn't hurt at all.

Later I put myself through a difficult course of learning about burns, stopping every ten minutes or so because I was having a panic attack.

I had the whole miserable spectrum of burns on various parts of my body, from first-degree all the way to fourth-degree. Before, I hadn't even known there were degrees.

You would think that the worst burns, third and fourth, would be the most painful, but that's not true. Thirds burn down through the whole of your skin, known as the dermis. Fourths burn down through the muscle, sometimes to the bone. In the past, few people survived fourths without immediate amputation.

But they don't hurt because they destroy the nerves in the skin. If you look down at yourself and see massive burn damage and you don't feel any pain, you are in deep trouble. Get yourself to a hospital, at once.

It's the firsts and seconds that cause the agony. I had a lot of those.

I learned about the Big Glitch in stages, reported to me by Gretel when she had returned from one of her forays Outside. That's how I began to think of it. Outside. The universe was divided into two more or less equal parts: my six-by-six-by-six cold universe of pain and everything else.

―――――――

At first I cursed the lack of an air lock on the shelter. Gretel had to come and go as time went on. After the third or fourth time, though, I hardly noticed it. Not long after that she finally located one of the things she had been looking for from the start. She returned from one of her scrounging expeditions with a mask that covered my face, and some extra oxygen bottles to feed it. After that, her comings and goings were less of an ordeal, though I still wouldn't recommend it the next time you go out into vacuum. She was able to improvise straps to hold the mask securely to my face—or what was left of it—for the fifteen seconds or so when there was no air for me to breathe. Though the pain of the mask was pretty bad, it was better than the sensation of air rushing from my lungs.

Eight days passed.

―――――――

Eight days? You gotta be kidding, don't you?

I wish I was.

For much of the first day, we waited to be rescued. But as the hours dragged by, it became more and more clear that we might be on our own, at least for a little while.

There was a small window in the pressure door, just a round bit of glass set into the metal.

The first time I noticed her looking, she quickly ducked down again.

"There's guys in pressure suits out there," she whispered. Whispering made no sense, of course, since even shouting through a bullhorn would not have carried through the vacuum outside.

"They're part of your bunch," she said. "Soldiers." She spat out that word with contempt. I wanted to tell her I hadn't signed up for anything like what actually went down, but who was I kidding? I had joined an invasion force, and it had not gone off according to plan.

"Are they looking this way?"

"I didn't get a good look. Should I look again?"

Carefully, she edged upward and peered through the glass.

"Okay, I see three soldiers. They're just standing around, it looks like. They're holding rifles, I guess. Not like the big laser you had." She looked back and down and glared at me. She looked back, and gasped.

"Two of them just picked up a body. He's in a uniform like the one you're wearing. They're going away from us, and now they're . . . oh, Chris, they just tossed the body on a stack of other ones. A *lot* of other ones. Soldiers. Civilians. Innocent bystanders, Chris. Are you happy?"

I had never been less happy but couldn't think of anything to say.

I think this was a few hours after we entered the shelter.

I know she had already made her first foray outside, and that time she had not seen anyone moving at all.

We know now that the soldiers had pulled back to regroup, and the Heinleiners had retreated to safety in places that appeared on no maps, pretty much beyond the reach of the invaders.

Gretel was getting increasingly antsy. There were things she needed to get, she told me. The air situation was not critical at that point. We debated whether or not to surrender to the people outside. She was in favor of it, in spite of their menacing appearance with the guns. And there was a risk that our refuge would be discovered anyway. We couldn't hide in there forever.

I was against it. I couldn't tell you exactly why. Maybe it was something to do with the Uglies, the mercenary troops from the Outer Planets. There had been something fishy about this operation from the first, but I had been too stupid to smell it.

"I don't care what you say, Chris. If I don't get you to a hospital, you're going to die. I'm going out there."

"Please, Gretel. Just give it one more hour." Something inside me was screaming to not let her leave as long as the soldiers were there. I even thought about trying physically to stop her, but clearly that would be impossible. She agreed, reluctantly, and sat down to pout about it. But the next time she looked outside, she found out how right I was.

"It's a couple of those bigger gorillas. They're walking up to the others . . . you said they were cops? There's about . . . three, four . . . I see six of them. The big guys are gesturing to them to . . ."

She screamed, and fell from her perch on the metal first-aid box. For quite a long time she wasn't able to find words. Finally she did.

"They're . . . *they're killing them!*" She screamed it over and over, approaching hysteria. I was utterly frustrated. There were so many things I wanted to do. Get up and look for myself. Go over and put my arm around her. Start screaming myself. But I had to keep my head if she was going to survive. After all she had done for me, it would be just the most terrible thing in the world if she died now.

"Calm down a little, Gretel. Who is killing who?"

It took awhile, but she finally was able to speak again.

"The big gorillas. They just started shooting at the other guys. You said they were cops, like you?"

"They must be. The big guys aren't part of us."

"Then who are they? Besides *murdering monsters!*"

"I'm not completely sure of that myself." There was no sense scaring her further by saying that they came from that legendary birthplace of monsters, Charon. "Look, Gretel, get up there and look again. See if they're doing a search." What we would be able to do about it if they were was a tough question. All I could come up with was for her to throw the door wide and make a run for it.

She didn't want to get back on the box. Who could blame her? But her bravery continued unabated. She edged up to it and pressed her eye to the glass.

"I don't see anything except . . ." She swallowed hard. "Some dead bodies. Six of them. Their suits are punctured, and there's . . ." She turned aside and vomited. "There's frozen blood all around them. They just *executed* them . . ." She began to lose it again. I managed to reach over and pat her leg. She calmed down a little.

"I don't see any of the monsters. I guess they didn't see us."

"Maybe they don't have the same kind of emergency shelters on Charon. Maybe they didn't recognize what it was."

"You think so?"

"I will if you will."

Later we learned what was going on. It was standard procedure for the Charonese when things went belly-up. They were eliminating witnesses who might be able to testify against them in an Interplanetary Court.

Each day that went by, we figured it could not last much longer. And then it lasted another day. No air outside, and no one moving around.

The lack of any sightings of Irontowners was a growing concern. Gretel fretted, unable to understand why none of her friends and family had repaired the damage to the environment and repressurized it. We still had no inkling of what was going on in the larger society, remember. We didn't know of the chaos that reigned everywhere, of the thousands and thousands of people who lost their lives because the CC became suicidal and went insane. There was no communication on either of our implanted techs. Mine could have been down because of the extensive damage to my head. We thought it was possible that the equipment had been fried, along with my face. But Gretel's should have worked.

I have since adjusted to a life without being connected to the grid. I no longer can just think a request and have an image pop up in my virtual vision. It's not as hard as you might imagine though I freely admit that it is inconvenient at times.

There was no food in the shelter, and very little water. We used up all the water on the first day, and were soon very thirsty. I stayed thirsty no matter how much water I drank. If I had more than a few sips, it would come right back up. The trouble was, with no air out there, much of the available water had boiled away. There had been a fountain not far from our shelter, but it was dry. The same with the spigots in the ice-cream parlor and other restaurants around the plaza. She was finally able to locate some five-gallon cans and schlep them back.

Finding food was easy enough. She was small and not very hungry. As the days went by, the stench of the two of us was enough to stun a brontosaurus. Or so she said. I smelled nothing. All I will say about our toilet arrangements was that she came back one day with a bucket. At least the bucket could be pretty much sterilized every time she went outside.

She couldn't do that with the other source of the stench, which was me. My flesh was putrefying.

Every time she left, I wished she would not come back. And every time she came back, I wished I could just die. But I don't seem to have suicide in me, and she was not a killer, even a mercy killer. And my body showed an amazing desire to cling to life.

The biggest problem in emergency situations though, as always in Luna, was air. The shelter had enough air for four to six people for about twenty-four hours. Do the math, and that's somewhere between around one hundred and one hundred fifty man-hours of air. Which should sustain the two of us for forty-eight to seventy hours. In reality, this one hadn't been serviced in a long time, and there was only about a third of full recommended pressure in the bottles. When Gretel discovered that, she used some words her mother probably wouldn't have approved of. We only had between sixteen to twenty hours of breathing. It didn't worry me, for myself, but I was desperate that Gretel should survive. And, of course, I couldn't do a damn thing about it.

There was another factor to consider. Though the null-suits were superior to the old helmet-and-suit variety of pressure suit, there was this about them: Without a connection to an exterior bottle slung over the back or shoulder, they were only good for about an hour. That was because there was only so much pressurized air you could fit into the lung-shaped internal bottle that took the place of the lung that was removed when the damn thing was installed.

I never knew exactly what Herculean tasks Gretel performed to keep us in air. She would leave and go scavenging, and somehow she found enough stuff to keep her alive and me barely ticking over.

Of course, what we both wanted her to do was explore, range far and wide and find someone to rescue us. But she was too busy scrounging most of the time. She refused to go out until it was absolutely necessary because of the toll we both knew the repeated exposures to vacuum were taking on me. Under the best conditions, she would only be able to range about for half an hour before she had to return and fill her tank again.

Eight days. Eight days like that.

I became increasingly delirious. She talked a lot, mostly to keep herself sane. She told me many things about her life, her family, her hopes and dreams. I remember only a little of that, and I won't share it with anybody, ever. That is between the two of us.

Then on the eighth day, someone knocked on the door. I don't remember it, but I'm sure Gretel almost jumped out of her skin. Was this a savior, or a killer?

An ambulance backed up to the pressure door and sealed itself against it. The door popped open. I do remember that, the door opening, light spilling inside, both of us blinking like troglodytes exposed to the sun for the first time. Gretel burst into tears. I wished I could, but I was too far gone.

A nurse later told me that I was as near death as anyone he had ever seen. The only thing I remembered for a long time was waking up once and discovering that the pain was gone.

So was much of my body. The list of things that needed replacing would have stretched to Mars and back. When the repair work is that extensive they bring you back to awareness gradually, so the next two weeks passed in a dreamlike state.

The first lucid experience I had was looking up from the treatment cell, wires and tubes webbing my body from legs to head, to see Gretel looking down on me. She was cleaned up, of course, and wearing clothes for the first time in a long time.

"How are you feeling?" she asked.

"I just want to thank you, for everything, but I don't know how I possibly could."

She shrugged.

"You would have done the same for me."

That's all I remember. She left. Later, I tried to find her, but she had vanished back into the secret world of libertarian Irontown.

After the passage of quite a few years, I gave up my search and accepted that I would probably never see her again.

They put me back together, just as good as new. They tried to talk me into getting new cyber implants, but I was adamant on the subject. The CC, or whatever took its place, was never getting into my head again.

It was my body they put together again, of course. As for my mind . . . that's still an ongoing project. It will probably never be reassembled just like it was. But I have learned to live with that.

SHERLOCK AGAIN

"You be a good dog while I'm away," αChris said to me. I could smell that he was worried. I played dumb by letting my tongue hang out and pretending I did not know where he was going. Playing dumb is not easy for me because I am very smart. I have learned that being smart and being clever are not the same thing. But I am also very clever as well as smart. A dog must be clever to pretend. I have learned how to pretend. Other dogs cannot pretend. They always wag their tails when they are happy or hang their heads when they are sad. I can wag my tail when I am sad. I can even wag my tail when I am angry! I am so clever!

I listened to αChris as he galumphed down the stairs. I love αChris with all my heart, but he could not sneak up on a newborn puppy. I cannot sneak as well as a damn cat, but who would want to be a damn cat?

When he was down to the dark street I hurried down the back stairs. I did not need to see him. I kept a good distance behind αChris as he started out toward Irontown. The spoor of αChris is the scent most familiar to me of the shitload of scents I know.

Does that make scents to you? Ha-ha!

———————

Some say that Irontown does not have a border. Some say that you gradually enter places that are more and more Irontown. This is like having your nose in the kitchen and your tail in the living room. Then you are in Irontown, and you did not even know you were there.

I have learned that this is not completely true. Maybe it is true for humans because humans are not very smart. There was a point in space that I passed and knew I was there. I marked that point in my mind. I began smelling things in combinations I had never smelled before. I began smelling things I had never smelled before at all. This was very interesting. I held my nose high, then low, and sucked up the smells.

Irontown smelled like . . .

(I have to interrupt Sherlock at this point. I tried to tell him that most of what he was saying made no sense to me, but he was having none of it. Smells are so important that he spent most of an hour listing them for me. By the time he was done, there had been

191

over two hundred *separate and distinct smells. I had names for fewer than fifty of them, and many of those I had to guess at. It was made all the more difficult because many of the smells were new to Sherlock, too. He knew precisely where to file them, to categorize them by similarity to other smells, or by who-knows-what system a dog has of classifying smells. Once more, it's a case of describing the ten thousand shades of "red" to a color-blind person.—PC)*

I did not like Irontown. I wished αChris did not have to go there to find Ms. Smith. Or now should I call her Ms. Shoes? It was confusing. I knew what shoes are. Dogs do not need shoes. I would not want to wear shoes. They look like they would hurt my paws.

I began seeing some of the people who lived in Irontown. Most of them looked and smelled like anybody else. But some of them were where the odd smells were coming from. And somewhere, behind some of the doors I passed, other smells were crowding into my nose.

I tracked αChris to a neighborhood, then to a corridor. Someone was cooking rice and chicken gravy. I like chicken gravy.

I followed αChris along the corridor. It got wide in some places and narrower in others. There were twists and turns. I was cautious when I came near the corners because I did not want αChris to know I was following him. I was afraid he might call me a bad dog. I hate that.

The sound changed before I went around the next corner. I listened, and I could tell that the corridor came to an end not far around that corner. I could hear shoes moving

slightly as someone ahead of me shifted himself. I thought
he was crouching; it sounded like that. I carefully edged up
to the corner and looked around. It was just as I thought.
There was αChris, squatting and looking at the thing that
listens to your radio voice and opens or locks the door.

I am such a good listener, as well as a good scenter!

I moved back around the corner. I could listen to what
was happening. I did not need to see what αChris was doing. If he started toward me, I would hear it and have plenty
of time to run back around the next corner.

I was not happy about following αChris like that. I want
to obey him, since he is the alpha. But I was worried that
he was going to get himself into trouble. αChris can sometimes rush into action when it might be smarter to sit back
and bark at it for a while. I have learned that when you rush
off by yourself, you sometimes end up with a wok full of
General Tso's chicken in your face and have to go to the
hospital. He should not go bumbling into trouble like a
puppy. But I cannot tell him that.

I heard music. I have very good ears, but I do not understand music. I do not understand why humans make the
noises they call music and listen to it. Some music is just
sounds. I have heard of things called harmonies, tempos,
tuning, and many other words humans use to describe music. I do not know what they mean. Some music has words.
Humans speak the words, but in a strange way that I do not
understand. It is called singing.

I heard music now. I understood some of the words. One

of the words was "money." I know what money is. I heard the numbers one two and three. I heard the word "cat." I hate cats. Then I heard the words "Blue Suede Shoes." I wondered, was this a song about our client?

Then I heard another song. Instead of a cat this song was about a dog. A hound dog. I know many kinds of hounds, but I do not know what kind of dog that is. Bloodhounds are the best kind of dog.

I heard αChris doing something at the door. This must be the door where Ms. Blue Suede Shoes lived. I peeked around the corner again and saw that he was still working at the lock. I hoped he did not get himself in trouble again. I have learned that going into someone's kennel without permission can get you in trouble.

There was a duffel bag sitting beside the door. I sniffed hard, but I could not tell what was in it from so far away. It got mixed up with the many other smells.

The door opened, and αChris went inside. I stayed back.

In a little while αChris came back outside, but he only picked up the duffel bag and took it back inside with him.

I decided to move a little closer. I would listen for αChris, and if I heard him coming out, I would run away.

When I got closer, I smelled old food that I have learned is Chinese food, like the General Tso's chicken. I also smelled fried corn tortillas, ground bronto, lettuce, tomato, jalapeno peppers, black pepper, lime juice, garlic, basil, oregano, and cilantro. I do not like cilantro. It tastes like soap. I have learned that these are things used in making salsa. I also smelled donuts. I like donuts as long as they are not the chocolate kind of donuts. I have learned that chocolate donuts are not good for dogs.

I smelled old flowers of the kind that are called daisies.

I heard αChris moving something around. I could not tell what it was. Then he dropped it back down.

For the first time I scented the woman who had called herself Mary Smith and who now called herself Ms. Blue Suede Shoes. I also smelled the feathers on the hat she had worn in our office.

Then the door at the end of the corridor opened and two men came through. The door was a thick door, which is known as a pressure door. I think that means it keeps the air inside. I think keeping the air inside is important because we all need air to breathe. Even damn cats.

I have always been taught by αChris that I should be polite to other people. I backed away from the door, but there was something about these men that I didn't like. Their sweat smelled like fear. But I backed away, like a good dog.

It was not very bright in the corridor. I was not trying to hide. I knew they saw me, but they paid no attention to me. I thought about going over to them to see if they were friendly to dogs. People who like dogs usually want to pet us. I do not mind being petted by strangers because αChris has taught me that I should let them do this. And it does feel good.

The men put things over their faces. I did not like this. I like to see the faces of people around me. I am able to tell many things about what humans are thinking when I can see their faces. Also their hands, and the way they stand. I have learned that all dogs can do this.

Then one of the men put his hands together and the other one stepped into the folded hands and was lifted up to an air grate high in the wall. He took something from his pocket and pried the grate off. Then he leaned inside. I heard something hissing.

The man jumped down and the other one went to the door. I felt the hair standing up on the back of my neck. Even though I am a clever dog who can wag my tail when I am angry, I am not able to keep the hair from standing up on the back of my neck when I am suspicious of something. I was very suspicious of these humans. I did not want them coming up behind αChris. I wanted to warn him. I took a deep breath and started to bark at them.

Then one of the men pulled the door shut.

αChris was inside the room. He was trapped.

I did not bark. I growled, and jumped on the man.

I bit him on the leg, then on the other leg—

(Here it is almost impossible to describe what happened next in consecutive terms. I have done my best, but Sherlock's thoughts during this time descended into a level that was much deeper than his conscious thoughts. One must remember that genetically Sherlock, like all dogs, is 99.96 percent wolf. From a Chihuahua to a Great Dane, even the most peaceful dog has, deep in his brain, the primitive instincts of his feral brother. When a dog is threatened, when his pack is threatened, the fight-or-flight reaction is triggered. Many domes-

ticated dogs choose flight, with their tails between their legs. They have simply had no experience of aggression. When outnumbered or facing a too-large opponent, wolves will flee, too. But when the odds are in their favor it is a different story. Something in Sherlock's brain looked at the situation and went on the attack.

(At that point his thoughts, even in remembrance, become far too bloodthirsty and alien to this particular peace-loving, nonaggressive, Homo sapiens; i.e., your humble narrator. The best I could do would be to string together words like Bite! Kill! Tear! Blood! Blood! Blood! Blood!

(And then . . . Hurting! Bite again! I am hit from behind! Hurting more! Must protect αChris! . . . but . . . hurting! Howl! Howl! Fear! Running, running, running .

(I also can't really translate the memory of fear, shame, humiliation, bewilderment, confusion, and agitation Sherlock was feeling as he abandoned the fight and ran away . . . because none of those words really express the canine emotions he broadcast to me. I know dogs better than most humans do, I know dogs better than I know most humans, but in the end, they are an alien species and there are gaps that will probably never be bridged. They will still be Canis and we will still be Homo.

(Now I can resume Sherlock's story from after the red bloodlust that briefly consumed him.—PC)

I bit the man.

I tried to kill him.

I know I am not supposed to, but it felt pretty good. I liked tasting his blood. Does that make me a bad dog?

I did not like running away. The other man hurt me,

and then the man I bit began to hurt me, too. The second man had a knife. It was not a big knife, but it went into my right hind leg, and I howled. I let go of the first man. I turned to face the second man. I know I snapped at the second man, but he stabbed at my face with his little knife.

Both of them were screaming and shouting, but I do not remember many of the words.

I remember one of them saying get the fucking dog off me.

I remember one of them saying kill it kill it kill it.

I remember one of them saying he tore my leg open.

That is all I remember. Then I ran down the corridor. I ran around the corner, then around another corner, and around another corner. I think I ran around one two three four five corners. Then I stopped.

I have learned that humans sometimes say they are licking their wounds. They do not really do this. αChris did not lick his wounds when he was burned and went to the hospital. I did lick my wound. I could not reach the cut on my head over my eye, but I could lick the deep stab wound on my leg. I tasted my blood. It was not exciting like it was to taste the man's blood. It tasted like fear.

The blood from the cut on my head was dripping into my eye. I shook my head until my ears flapped, but the blood still flowed.

I did not know what to do. I sat down and whined. I had failed αChris. I had failed the pack. I had run away from pain and danger. No wolf would have run away from those two men. A wolf would have torn the throats out of those two men. A wolf would have howled his victory to the rest of the pack. I wanted to howl. But it would not be a howl of victory. It would be a howl of shame.

I was a failure. I was no wolf. I was just a sad bloodhound. I did not feel clever at all. I was a bad, bad, bad dog.

(A note on Sherlock's feelings of shame. Many humans would have felt the same after what happened and what he did. But I have learned that dogs feel shame in a different way than humans do. They feel it intensely, probably even worse than humans do. If you have ever seen a dog who has made a mess and been caught at it, you might get an idea of what I'm talking about. Call him a bad dog and he will lower himself to the ground and grovel at your feet.

(But they get over it more quickly than a human would. Where many people would brood over such a thing for many hours, or possibly even days or weeks, a dog can usually shake it off in little more than a few minutes. There seems to be a shut-off mechanism somewhere in the canine mind that tells him something like "Well, that sucked, but it's over now. Let's move on." Water under the bridge. That bird has flown. Forget it. Fuck it.

(I mention this to account for how very quickly Sherlock put all that behind him, stopped licking his wounds, and jumped once more unto the breach.—PC)

My leg hurt, but I could ignore it. A wolf would ignore it. I would be a wolf until I was back with αChris. Yes, I *would* be a wolf! But I would be a crafty wolf. They say foxes are sly. I would be like a fox, too.

I hurried back around one two three four corners, and

slowed down before looking around the next corner. I
wanted to charge back into the fight. I wanted to take the
two men by surprise. I wanted to come up behind them
and bite them on the ass. But I was like a fox. I leaned forward and looked around the last corner.

The men had done something to the lights in the corridor. It was very dim. I think they did not want the people
in the other apartments to see what they were doing. But
that would be good for me. I have learned that although
humans see colors that I cannot see, my eyes in the dark are
a lot better than human eyes are.

I saw the men open the door of Mary Smith's apartment
and go inside. I crept along the corridor, past one two three
four five and more doors to other apartments. No one came
out of these doors.

I reached the door where I had last seen αChris, the door
to Mary Smith's apartment. I looked inside. It was even
darker in there, but I could see the two men picking up
αChris, one at his head and the other at his feet. I felt the hair
standing up on the back of my neck again. I forgot all about
being a fox, and I sprang through the door and onto them.

I smelled something I had never smelled before. I like
almost all smells, but I did not like this one. I have learned
that I was smelling something the men had sprayed into the
air, something called knockout gas. I did not know that
then, though.

They dropped αChris and started shouting again. I bit
one of them on the leg . . . and then I let go. I had lost all

my strength. I felt myself going to sleep. I did not want to go to sleep. I wanted to stay awake and help αChris, but I felt my eyes closing.

One of the men said goddamn dog but the gas got him. The other said let's get the fuck out of here. And I think he said I didn't sign up to get my fucking leg torn off.

The men carried αChris out of the apartment. I wanted to stay awake, I wanted to get up, but I was very weak. I could not understand it. I tried to think of some way to stay awake. I had an idea, and I was very proud of myself. I was a clever dog once again!

I twisted around and bit my leg where the bloody wound was. It hurt very badly, but I did not care. I suddenly felt very awake. I tried not to whine, and I tried to get up, but my legs would not get me up. So I crawled.

The smell of the knockout gas was not so strong, and I staggered to my feet as I reached the door. I looked to one side and saw the back of one of the men go through the door at the end of the corridor. The door was swinging closed behind him.

I knew I had to hurry. This door was not the kind of door that is opened with a card. This was a door with an old-fashioned door latch. If it shut completely, I would be helpless. Dog paws cannot turn a door latch. I would have to find someone to open the door for me.

I dashed toward the door. In the faint light of the corridor the closing door was a line of light that got narrower and narrower. I was still not completely awake, but I managed to get there in time to stick one paw in the gap between the door and the frame. It hurt. The door kept trying to close, but my paw was in the way. I could not take my paw away, or the door would close completely.

I am not good at telling time. I do not know how long I scratched at the door with my other paw until I got it opened wide enough to stick my nose in. It seemed like a very long time.

(Given how far away the men had traveled before Sherlock got the door open, I estimate it was five minutes. During that time he injured himself in many places on both front paws and his face and ears, trying to fit a large dog through a small opening.—PC)

After a while I managed to get through the door. On the other side of it there were stairs. I like stairs that go up. I do not like stairs that go down as much, but usually they are okay. But that day I was hurting in both my front legs and one of my hind legs. I hoped that the men who had taken αChris had gone up the stairs. I would have been happier to go up the stairs.

They were going down the stairs.

I could just barely hear them down there, clumping about, but the sound was very faint. But even if I had been deaf, I would have known they were going down because that is where the scent trail led.

I started down the stairs.

There were one two three four five a whole shitload of stairs. There would be some stairs going one way, then a landing, then more stairs going the other way. And then more stairs going the other other way, and more stairs going the other other other way.

This went on for a very long time. A shitload of time. One two three four five shitloads of time. Every step hurt my front paws. Every step hurt my cut hind leg. Blood leaked into my eye until it dried and my eyelid stuck closed. Then the blood stopped flowing. I wanted to stop and lick my wound, but every time I stopped for a breath I could hear the men below still going down, but getting so faint I could hardly hear them over my own breathing. I had to keep going. αChris needed me.

Then once when I stopped I heard a door slam shut down below. Then I did not hear anything except my own breathing and my own heartbeat. I did not remember ever hearing my heart beating so fast. My heart went bump *bump!* bump *bump!* bump *bump!*

But I had to move on. I could hear myself whimpering with every step I took downward. I did not want to whimper, but I could not stop myself. I asked myself, would a wolf whimper? Maybe a wolf *would* whimper. Wolves are just dogs with a bad attitude.

You know what? *Fuck* wolves! I was a dog, and I would keep going, no matter what. Dogs have stood beside humans since we all lived in caves, or up in trees, or wherever we used to live on that place they call Old Earth. We tracked foxes, herded sheep, found live birds, fetched dead birds, helped humans who could not see or hear, chased and caught bad humans, protected humans, smelled out many things, and pulled sleds through snow.

I have seen all these things on the television.

I finally got to the bottom of the stairs. Someday I would like a human who understands numbers to tell me just how many steps I went down. I would not understand the number, but it would be nice to know.

At the bottom of the stairs, there was another door. This was not a doorknob door, but a good door. I could find my way past this door. I went to the place in my head and tried several things, but nothing happened.

I tried more things, and still nothing happened. I wanted to sit down and howl at something. I have learned that dogs used to howl at the moon, but αChris and I live on the moon. So what could I howl at? This was a problem that I decided to set aside to think about later.

The door was in a wall that was one wall of a corridor that stretched out in both directions on either side of me. I could not see the end in either direction. I knew I had to go one way or the other, but which way?

I was half-blind and limping, but my very, very smart nose was still working as well as it always did. So I began casting back and forth, trying to pick up a scent that might help me decide which way to go.

And I picked up the faintest, faintest . . .

(Once again Sherlock enters into realms that I, or any human,

can't really appreciate. The way he thought of this faint scent feels to me like it might have been something like one molecule of αChris scent in a million, but it might have been a billion, or a trillion. I simply can't quantify it. But whatever it was, it was only in one direction, which I believe was to the left, though Sherlock was sometimes a little vague about left and right.—PC)

I set off after the scent. I did not know how a bit of αChris's skin could have come through the solid wall beside me, but I knew that was what it was.

There were lights in the ceiling, but not all of them worked, and some of them flickered. I did not like the flickering. It confused me. But I kept on, sniffing the air. The scent never got very strong, but it was there. I splashed through puddles and under drips from the ceiling. The water smelled of oil and very old concrete and rusting steel.

I came to a ventilation grate set low, near the floor. It was hanging loose, but there was not enough room for me to squeeze through. I smelled αChris stronger coming from that air grate, so I squeezed through anyway. The edges of the grate tore at my skin. I smelled fresh blood. I do not like to smell my own fresh blood. It makes me want to run away.

But I did not run. The scent was coming from the direction where I had just been. The corridor was just on the other side of the air duct. I had to duck my head and crouch a little to move along the duct. This was not easy with my sore paws and leg, but I kept going.

I followed many turns in the air duct. The scent got stronger, then weaker. I turned back many times and turned into a different branch. I have a very good sense of direction, but I was getting confused. I tried to look at the map in my head, but this place was out beyond the edge of that map. I tried to find other maps, but I could not do that.

The scent got even more faint. I had to inhale very deeply, and inhale many times, before I could pick up just a little of it. Then I could no longer be sure that I was smelling αChris at all.

I finally entered a much larger air duct. One two three four five humans could have walked side by side along this air duct. And the scent of αChris got a little stronger. I tried to run in the direction of the scent, but I could not run. My legs would not take me any faster. I smelled more blood. But I kept going.

(Here Sherlock's memories get vague and jumbled again. If dogs can get delirious—the results are not completely in on that—he was getting punchy. His pain must have been intense. But his determination was even stronger.

(And I must say that, much as I thought I knew the minds, the capabilities, of a CEC, Sherlock surprised me and deeply moved me. Because he showed me that CECs are advanced enough that they actually have a concept of death. It's a confused and muddled one . . . but I could say the same of my own take on the conundrum of mortality. I suspect that, unless you are a deeply committed Presleyite or Mormon or Christian or Muslim, your ideas about death are pretty uncertain, too.

(Here is the best I can do at decoding the thoughts that ran through Sherlock's dog brain as he told me the story.——PC)

I have been told that animals cannot understand death. I have been told that all animals flee pain, but it is just pain they are trying to avoid, not death. I have learned elephants visit the bones of their dead pack mates. That they seem to mourn them. But do they know that the dead elephant no longer exists?

I have seen dead animals. They get cold, and they soon smell different. It is hard to understand that the dead animals used to be living animals. That they used to eat and breathe and shit. The dead animals had wants and needs, and now they do not want or need anything.

I believe that animals can look at the dead body of another animal like themselves and maybe understand that the dead body will not move again. But I have learned that some animal mothers will hold on to their dead puppies for days. But others will abandon the dead puppy quickly. When an animal sees the dead body of an animal like themselves, do they understand that one day they will be a dead body, too? Everyone says no.

Humans understand that one day they will be dead. I am a supersmart dog, and I understand that one day I will be dead, too. But it does not make any sense to me. How can I be a nondog? How can I be a non-Sherlock?

I thought that I was dying. I did not want to die, but I did not have the strength to keep on living. I could not keep moving.

My nose told me that I was deeper into Irontown than I had ever been before. There were new smells that I had never smelled before. But I was too confused to figure out what they were.

I took deep breaths. I hoped that the deep breaths would bring life back into my body. But I was still too tired to get up.

I could no longer smell αChris. I had no idea which way to go even if I could get up and walk.

I took one more breath. I smelled the faintest trace of something stronger and more pungent than the smell of αChris's skin. I knew I had smelled it before. I knew I had smelled it not long ago.

It was the smell of knockout gas. It was the smell of knockout gas clinging to αChris's clothes and skin.

I lifted my head.

I got to my feet.

I set off to find the source of the knockout gas.

seventeen _____

"If I see that fucking dog again, I'm gonna kill it."

"Don't talk like that. We had our orders."

"Yeah? Did you hear anyone warn us about the hound from hell? Did anyone mention that I might lose my balls?"

"Shut up. The dog never bit you on the balls. It would have been a lucky bite, anyway. How would he have found them?

"Very funny. You're not the one who's still bleeding."

"Don't be a crybaby. You're barely scratched."

"Barely scratched? Fuck you, Tom. That fucking monster bit right down to the bone. Soon as we get this joker squared away, I'll show you."

"I think I'll skip that great pleasure."

"Besides, who is it that stuck the knife into the dog?"

"That was a mistake, I'll admit it. He surprised me."

"You think it wasn't a surprise to me, when he clamped down on my thigh, right up near the scrotum?"

They went on like that for a while. They couldn't seem to stop bickering.

All I was getting was sound. I couldn't seem to open my eyes. I couldn't move my arms or legs, either. I was blind and paralyzed. I guess my ears were the first thing I got back because there is no muscle movement involved in hearing.

I was scared. What had they done to me?

———

I later learned their real names, but I won't reveal those. Let's just call them Tom and Jerry.

I was being carried, with Tom at my feet and Jerry at my shoulders. I had all the strength of an overcooked noodle. I could feel myself flopping around uselessly. It's a terrible feeling.

I understand that back in the days when blindness was usually permanent, either from birth or disease or accident, blind people were said to have developed very sensitive hearing. I can vouch for that. Even having been blind for probably no more than ten minutes, I found that I could detect more things about my surroundings than I would have thought possible. Different spaces produce different reverberations. When I first woke up I was sure I was being carried down a standard corridor, possibly the very one I had traveled to get to the apartment where I had been gassed. That went on for a while, then we moved into a larger space. I'm not saying that my ears could tell me just how big it was, but I knew it was significantly bigger. There was background noise, but I couldn't identify any of it except that I got the impression it was industrial.

Then we were back in a corridor, and it felt like this one was narrower. Then we entered what I was sure was a room. Not a corridor, not a public space, not a factory. A room.

I was thrown unceremoniously onto a soft, yielding surface. A bed or a couch. I managed to crank one eye open a little bit.

"He's coming to," Tom said. I could see his head hovering over me, a blurry cartoon balloon with features badly painted on it. Or maybe it was Jerry. Then the other one leaned over me. *Two* cartoon balloons.

"Hey, asshole," the balloon said. "Don't you know there are laws about keeping vicious dogs? I should have killed the damn thing."

"If you do," I said, "I will skin you alive and throw the rest of you into a garbage compactor."

Or that's what I intended to say. What I actually said was more like "Goo poo skurkle booty goo foo *goo*!" I could only hope that the tone of my voice made my meaning plain.

"Screw you, too, asshole," he said back.

"Let's get out of here. We got more work to do."

"Fine, as soon as I make a trip to the walk-in medico. I've lost a lot of blood. I'm feeling faint."

"Don't you pass out on me; I'm tired from schlepping his deadweight. No way I'm gonna carry you."

And with that, the comedy team of Tom and Jerry left. I heard an old-fashioned key turning in an old-fashioned lock. And me without my handy private eye set of picklocks.

I felt like crying. I wondered where I was. But that was secondary.

Mostly, I wondered where Sherlock was.

———————

It was hours before I could get up and move around my prison cell. I spent them looking around, first by moving my eyes, then my whole head, then actually sitting up.

I say prison cell, but it actually wasn't all that bad. It was nothing like the cells you see in old film noir. It looked old. There were rivets holding the metal sheets together. The paint was battleship gray, and flaking off in places. Later, when I could get up and walk around, I tried picking at those places within my reach, but it was no good. The metal underneath was perfectly sound. I would need a cutting torch to get through the walls.

Though still weak and woozy I got up and paced out the dimensions of my cell. It was an odd shape. Tom and Jerry had thrown me onto a bunk that would have looked right at home in a children's camp cabin in one of the disneylands. It was the bottom bunk of three, and there were four other three-deckers around the room. There were twelve lockers, and a kitchenette with a microwave and a coffeemaker and a can opener and basic tableware in drawers. A small door, the only one that would open, led to a toilet, sink, and shower all squeezed into a small space.

There was one peculiarity that it took me awhile to understand. The furniture and even the kitchen counters were built so that they could be removed and attached to the walls. The bathroom was mounted on a gimbal arrangement. It could rotate through ninety degrees.

I was in a cabin on a spaceship.

———————

It took ten minutes to learn all there was to learn about my quarters. After that, time stretched out. I had very little to do.

First, I satisfied myself that the door was not going to be opened with a harsh look. It was solidly set in its frame. It was a pressure door, fitting seamlessly into its rubber gaskets. I tried looking through the keyhole, but the lock was not *that* old-fashioned. There would be no through-and-through hole in a pressure door.

I took a metal fork from the kitchen and tried probing the lock and ended up with a fork with a bent tine. I hadn't held out much hope of opening it, but it was still discouraging.

I couldn't think of anything to do after that but sit on my thumbs.

———————

There was no way of telling how long I was there before I heard the door lock turn and the slight hiss of pressure equalizing.

"Hey, you in there. Stand back from the door."

"Hey yourself. Let me out of here!"

"Can't do it, mate. You wanna eat, or not? It's all the same to me."

I wasn't really very hungry, but any change at all would be a good thing, so I stepped back to the far wall.

"Who are you?" I asked. "Why are you doing this to me?"

"Questions, questions, questions. All in good time."

"Dammit, what are you going to do with me? Who are you? Where am I? Is this a spaceship?"

"Still with the questions. Ask me what's for dinner, I'll tell you that." He took the cover off the tray and the smells suddenly made me ravenous. I felt like I could eat a whole brontosaurus ham, and a side of ribs, too.

"Cow steak smothered in hollandaise sauce and sautéed mushrooms," he said, "with crispy deep-fried chips, a side of broccoli au gratin, chocolate milk, and a slice of key lime pie."

"Please thank the chef," I said, with a sneer.

"That would be me. Sorry about the milk, it was all I could find at the moment."

"Next time have a steward bring the wine list."

He turned and started to go. I had the tray in my hand,

and I thought about hurling it at him and trying to make it to the door. He wasn't a big guy, and I figured I could take him if I had to . . .

. . . but I was still not at my best. Also, I'd like to have a better idea what was beyond that door. An empty corridor, or fifteen well-armed guards?

Plus, I was really hungry. Get some food in me, and I'll think about hurling the breakfast tray.

"Hey, man, please give me a break. How long are you going to keep me in prison?"

He turned back.

"This is not a prison."

"Great. Then I'll be leaving now, thank you."

His mouth twisted up a bit.

"All right, you're being detained. I really don't know how long it will be."

"Okay. Where's my dog? I'm sure I heard him just before you guys knocked me out. What happened to Sherlock?"

Now he looked angry. He pulled up his pant leg and showed me some pink, freshly healed wounds. Some of them looked like tooth marks.

"Your goddamn dog! He practically tore off my leg!"

"He wouldn't have done that unless you gave him a very good reason. You were kidnapping me, don't forget that."

"'Kidnapping' is a pretty harsh word. It's for your own good, believe me. One day you'll thank us."

"Damn you, tell me what happened to my dog!"

This time he looked a bit uncomfortable.

"He was okay the last time I saw him. That is . . ."

"What?"

"Well, we might have had to stab him a little, in the leg, to make him let go." He actually shuffled his feet a little. "Look, man, I'm a dog lover, too. I got a little Pomeranian, cute as the dickens. But what would you do if a huge hound like that was trying to kill you?"

He actually had a point, but I wasn't about to tell him that.

"Look, man, just let me out. Okay? I promise I won't go to the cops. I don't know who you are. I don't know where I am. You can blindfold me and take me someplace and let me go. What could I tell them?"

For a moment I thought he was thinking it over, but that was not to be. He shook his head and turned to go again.

"What is your Pom's name?"

That stopped him.

"Trixie."

"What would you think if you knew Trixie was out there somewhere, with a stab wound in her leg? How would you feel? My dog's name is Sherlock, by the way."

"I'd feel terrible." He sighed. "Look, Mr. Bach . . . I'll put the word out to look for an injured bloodhound. That's the best I can do. Maybe someone can catch him and treat him. But last I saw him, he was running away with his tail between his legs. I'll bet he ran a long, long way."

That didn't sound like Sherlock, but what did I know? The poor guy had never really been in a fight-or-flight situation. He might have run away.

Tom went outside and shut the door behind him. On the off chance, I went to the door and tried the knob. I was not surprised to find it was locked.

———

A prison cell with five-star cuisine. How crazy was that?

A bit of an exaggeration, but it was all very good. Tom was a first-rate chef, I had to give him that. So what was he doing acting as a kidnapper and a jailer? Moonlighting?

The walls closed in around me again. Eventually Tom appeared again, this time bearing eggs Benedict. With sides of hash browns, extracrispy bacon, a hot buttered English muffin, and a large glass of orange juice.

"So is it morning outside? How long have I been in here?"

"Almost twenty-four hours."

That was longer than I had ever been away from Sherlock. I was so worried about him I could hardly think straight.

"Hey, I'm going out of my mind with boredom. Every prison movie I ever saw, the inmates get to leave their cells for exercise now and then. How about it? A deck of cards so I can play solitaire. Or you can join me if you want and we can play gin rummy."

"I told you, this isn't a prison."

"Well, a cage by any other name . . . come on. A book or two? A screen so I can watch old movies?"

"I'll see what I can do."

———————

What he could do was a dilapidated player. It wouldn't pick up any current shows or news, but the crystal had several hundred thousand movies and shows in the archive. There were even a few I hadn't seen.

I began counting off the days with hash marks, in the time-honored manner of jailbirds everywhere. I made a mark on the wall every time breakfast was served.

Soon I had fifteen marks on the wall.

The player saved me from going crazy. I unrolled the screen and started going through the menu. I looked at a lot of jailbreak movies, and a lot of black-and-white noir. I had seen many of them before.

In the film of Raymond Chandler's *Farewell, My Lovely*, Robert Mitchum as Philip Marlowe is drugged and locked up in a private sanatorium in Bay City. It is run by a beefy broad named Frances Anthor. Marlowe clocks her a good one with his fist; it does him no good.

But someone gets careless, and Marlowe staggers out of the place through a scene of violent chaos.

Could I do the same? I still had no idea of what was beyond that door, but I might never find out if I just lay back and took it all.

What Marlowe does is overpower the attendant. So one evening—it had to be evening, Tom had told me the entree was pasta primavera—I waited by the side of the door and when it opened, I upended the tray out of Tom's arms and up into his face.

Tom looked surprised and hurt, and then I was past him and out the door.

He might have been careless, but he was a lot quicker than I had expected. I got one short look at a long corridor with doors opening to either side, then I was overcome with what must have looked like an epileptic seizure. I'd seen them in the movies. I never passed out, but I was totally helpless. I watched as Tom pocketed the taser, then he leaned over and shook his finger at me. He said nothing but dragged me back to the room. There were noodles all over his face and chest.

Breakfast the next morning was cold oatmeal and a stale bun. It went like that for three days, then he relented with a really great Caesar salad and roasted veggies. Tom just couldn't resist being a good cook.

I marked off twenty-five days.

———————

Prison routine can be so stultifying that when something changes, it can throw you for a loop.

One morning, Tom showed up to collect my breakfast tray and there was someone with him. Call him Dick. He was enormous, and carried what looked like an electric shock stick, colloquially known as a cattle prod. He slapped it into his palm a few times.

"Are you going to give me any trouble, Mr. Bach?" he asked.

"Not a bit," I said. "In fact, we're going to be friends, so you can call me Chris."

Dick looked at Tom.

"Is he trying to be funny?"

"He t'inks he's a private gumshoe, always makin' wit' da wisecracks. A wiseguy, dat's what he is."

Okay, Tom had boned up on the old lingo as a counterattack to my attempts at sarcastic tough-guy dialogue. Donuts were sinkers. Coffee was joe. Milk was moo juice. Toast was a raft. Butter was axle grease. I found it as annoying as he must have found my lame bits of dialogue. What he didn't know was that I acted the tough guy so I could almost convince myself that I wasn't scared.

"No, no trouble," I said, quietly.

"Turn around, face the wall, hands behind your back."

He cuffed me and slipped a hood over my head. I tried to control my breathing, but the heartbeat was racing away. Each of them took me by an elbow and walked me out of the room. It all had the air of being marched to an execution. I hoped that was just my imagination running away with me.

Then we stopped, and they took the hood off. I looked all

around. I managed to look behind me and saw a big air lock. I knew it was the standard sort used for cargo on freighter ships. So I had been right. My cell had been aboard a ship.

But where we were now was airtight, too, which means stuff had been built right up to the side of the huge ship, tight as a barnacle on an ocean liner. And I recognized where I was. It was an open plaza in Irontown.

The fact that they didn't care that I saw the ship or the Irontown space scared me. If a kidnapper lets you see his face, it probably means you are not going to survive the experience. I had worried about that during the twenty-five days of my imprisonment; but Tom was such an amiable, harmless-seeming guy that I had a hard time taking it seriously. Now, with the appearance of Dick, I wasn't so sure.

But what really scared me had little to do with what was happening now. I recognized this place though it was much changed. This was the mall where I had been burned to a crisp. That realization weakened my knees so much that Dick had to catch me and get me back to my feet.

They took me across the open space, bustling with people. We approached a small restaurant with delicate twisted-metal chairs and tables outside. There was a lovely woman seated at one of the tables. People were coming and going, asking questions and getting quick, brusque answers. There was a hot-fudge sundae on the table beside her, and she took a spoonful as I got nearer, then glanced up at me and smiled.

I saw the sign on the wall behind her. Aunt Hazel's Ice Cream Emporium.

The woman got to her feet, then she looked alarmed. I heard a commotion behind me and turned around to see what was happening.

A pack of twenty or so dogs was coming at us, full speed, growling. In the lead was Sherlock.

eighteen _____

SHERLOCK

Spike said <I sniff your ass.> And he did that.

Lassie said <I think he will be okay, αSpike.>

I said <I roll over and show you my belly.> And I did that.

Rin Tin Tin said <He is hurt, αSpike.>

(This will be a little difficult to explain.

(Sherlock limped deeper into Irontown, dazed and confused, though the bleeding had stopped. He doesn't remember a lot from that time until he stumbled onto a pack of wild dogs.

(It could only happen in Irontown. In the rest of the world, runaway or abandoned dogs and other pets are quickly rounded up by bobbies and either returned to their owners, adopted out, or euthanized. But the Heinleiners and other Irontown residents

were so dedicated to the idea of minding one's own business that
so long as a dog didn't bite someone or crap in the public walk-
way or make a nuisance of herself in some other way, they let her
alone. They even set out food and water for these feral animals.
Individual dogs would often bond with a human who treated
them kindly and leave the street life. But others chose to remain
wild and free. The pack Sherlock encountered was composed of such
animals. But there was one crucial difference. Many of them were
CECs.

(Sherlock has seldom socialized at all, and never with another
CEC. He was hardly prepared for what that was like. By interfacing
with the computers they were able to communicate in a way that
was sort of like telepathy. And it presented some real challenges for
me, as the interpreter.

(Obviously they did not speak to each other in words. But they
were able to convey ideas and, especially, feelings in a way that no
dogs had ever done before. They could share fairly complex information with each other. As an example, when Sherlock first found the
pack, they saw that he was hurting badly. The alpha, αSpike, a
Dalmatian, and the rest of the pack knew where there was a veter-
inarian who would treat dogs. They told Sherlock this, guided him
to the right place, and scratched on the door. He collapsed on the
floor once he was inside.

(The vet's name was Sorenson, and she knew that some of the
αSpike pack were CECs. She had some experience of them and was
able to learn from αSpike that Sherlock had a master, but was
separated from him. The dogs were not able to make her understand
that Chris Bach had been kidnapped and was in trouble, but she

did understand that Sherlock did not want to find a new home. He just wanted to be treated and released. She agreed, treated and bound up his wounds, injected him with some substance that energized him considerably, gave him a Bowser Bow-wow Bacon-flavored Doggie Snack, and sent him on his way.

(And the great search for αChris was under way.——PC)

αSpike said <Not so fast. Sherlock, Rule Number One is that I, Spike, am alpha. Will you submit?>

I said <I am on my back.>

αSpike said <Good. Rule Number Two Three Four and Five is that I, αSpike, am alpha.>

I stayed on my back. I said <You are alpha, αSpike.>

αSpike said <Good. Rule Number Six is do not shit or piss on the public street. Do not mark your territory. Use the dirt patches provided. I will define our territory. Do you agree to this?>

I said <I do, αSpike.>

With that, I was accepted into the pack.

I was happy that the vet, Dr. Sorenson, took care of my stabbing wound. She also put some medicine on my other scrapes and bruises. Then I departed with αSpike and the rest of our pack.

I did not know I could talk to other dogs. The voices and pictures in my head had always been cold and without feeling. But when I was with the pack, voices and feelings were warm and welcoming.

It was a good pack. But I could only talk to some of this pack.

αSpike was the pack alpha, and I submitted to him without question. I did not want to fight any battles with αSpike or anyone else. All I wanted to do was look for αChris. Also, although I am a very smart dog, I could see at once that αSpike was even smarter. αSpike could count to one two three four five . . . and up to twenty. That is how many dogs were in the pack. Twenty. That is a large pack, I think.

Not all the pack were smart like me. Here are the smart ones:

αSpike, a Dalmatian.

Sarah, a golden retriever. She was the alpha bitch. *(Sherlock's word, again, and I will not use it again.——PC)*

Fritzi, a Doberman female.

βRin Tin Tin, the beta male.

Lassie, a collie. When I sniffed her ass I could tell she had recently been in heat, and was now going to have some puppies.

Oskar, a Rottweiler who was always looking for a chance to challenge αSpike for pack leader. I steered clear of him.

Then there were the dumb ones. These ordinary dogs hung out with us but they were not a part of our plans. They were a Chihuahua named Pedro, a Papillon named Henri, a Jack Russell terrier female named Jackie, and an Irish setter named Colleen. There were others but I do not know their names. Jackie and Pedro were always yapping around and making nuisances of themselves until Oskar snapped at them. That would shut them up for a little while. But they could not help themselves, and were soon running underfoot again. I have learned that a word for dogs like that is "high-strung."

Our names came from our masters, like my name of Sherlock. I was named Sherlock by αChris. But most of the other smart dogs did not come from happy homes like I did. αSpike and Lassie and Rin Tin Tin and Oskar had escaped from a place called a laboratory, where humans had been doing experiments on them. I do not really understand what that means, but I do understand that the way of making dogs like me supersmart came from laboratories. I think that that is why αSpike is supersupersmart. They did something to him.

———————

Lassie was the CEC dog who had a good clock in her head. She knew what time it was. She knew when we could find good things to eat.

Lassie said <It is the day when the house special at Tony's trattoria is five-cheese ravioli with clam sauce.>

Fritzi said <I like five-cheese ravioli with clam sauce!>

The others all agreed that Tony's five-cheese ravioli with clam sauce was very good food.

Lassie said <It is now closing time at Tony's trattoria. Tony will have a bucket of scraps. I am hungry.>

The rest of the pack agreed that they were hungry, too.

αSpike said <We will go to Tony's trattoria and feast on scraps.>

Rin Tin Tin led the way. I learned that he had the best map in his head. I had no map in my head because we were in Irontown. But as we moved through Irontown, a map grew in my head. One day I might be able to find my way to places like Tony's trattoria by myself.

The pack found our way to an alley that ran behind Tony's trattoria. There were bins of garbage that smelled interesting. Tony came out the back door with a big bucket in one hand and a stack of steel dishes in the other. He set down the bucket and then he scratched αSpike behind the ears. αSpike tolerated this. I felt αSpike's feelings, and I understood that αSpike did not like humans very much, but he knew how to get along with them. Then Tony started setting the dishes down.

Tony said, "I scraped all the food folks left on their plates into the bucket. Lots of 'em tonight. Plus a lot of stale bread and some meat that I can't sell. But you ladies and tramps don't mind, do you?"

He scraped the food into the dishes and went back inside.

αSpike went to a bowl and started to eat. We held back, then slowly approached the other bowls. The alpha always eats first, all dogs know that. But stupid little Pedro tried to eat from αSpike's dish. Spike growled at him and nipped his ear. Pedro squeaked like a little mouse and ran away.

After Oskar had eaten, I sniffed at what was left in the bowl, and ate that. But a few minutes later, it came back up.

Sarah said <Are you through with that?>

I said that I was, and she ate it.

The pack had a den where we could all spend the night. It was near a heating duct, so it was warm. I liked the warm air. It made my sores feel better. We huddled together, the smarties in one group and the dummies in another. I told them that I had not run away from αChris, my master.

I told them that I loved my master and that I wanted to find him.

I told them about all the good things αChris had done for me. I told them about being a private detective and about how αChris and I were partners. I told them how we went looking for people.

The smarties from the laboratory were very impressed. The smarties who had escaped from bad masters were also impressed. None of them had ever had a master who cared for them. None of them had ever had anything to do except look for food.

The laboratory smarties had grown up without the love of a human. They wished they knew what it felt like to be partners with a human. I tried to tell them. The laboratory smarties had grown up in small cages. They were smart, and so they were bored. There was nothing for them to do. αSpike was supersupersmart, and so he was even more bored than the others. He knew that even the dummies in the pack were bored if they did not have something interesting to do.

αSpike said <We must help Sherlock find this Chris human.>

229

The other smarties agreed this would be a good thing to do. They were ready to go out sniffing at once.

αSpike said <Not yet. I must think about this a little more. I am supersupersmart, and I am alpha, so you must do what I tell you to do.>

Everyone agreed that this should be so.

Spike said <I think better when I am doing something. We will all go to the park now and chase some balls.>

Everyone sat up and was excited at the idea of chasing balls. I was excited, too, but I knew I was still too sore to chase balls.

In the park, someone who loved dogs had set up a machine that threw balls far across the green grass in the park. I have learned that these balls were called tennis balls. I watched my pack chasing balls. When they captured them, they brought them back and dropped them back into the machine.

It looked like fun. But I wanted to find αChris. That was all I could think about. I hoped the game would end soon.

The game did end, and Lassie told us where the next good place to find food was. I do not remember where it was, but we knocked over some bins to get the food. I ate some bread with bits of cheese and ham, and I did not vomit this time.

———————

Later we went back to our den.

Spike said <Now tell us about this human, Chris.>

Oskar said <What does he smell like?>

I told them . . .

(This is probably the part that is the least translatable of all the things I heard from Sherlock. Even dogs can't describe to each other how one specific human smells. But Sherlock was able to say quite a few things that were part of Chris's smell. Sherlock said it was a "shit-load" of smells. None of them meant anything to me and they won't mean anything to you, but as before, telling me how Irontown smelled, Sherlock would not just skip over it because of my scent-blindness. And amazingly, if Sherlock is to be believed, he managed to communicate a pretty good idea of the scent the pack should be sniffing for.—PC)

The days went by beyond my counting. They went by beyond even αSpike's counting, and αSpike can count to twenty.

Irontown was bigger than αChris had known. We sniffed out many humans who smelled something like αChris, but every time one of the pack would bring me to smell him, it was not αChris.

The map inside my head grew and grew. We went to the edges of Irontown, and beyond into the mapped world. This was dangerous since there were dogcatchers when we left Irontown. Little Pedro was not quick enough to escape them. One day I looked back and saw him being picked up by a female human in a uniform. He was barking and barking and barking, but it did not do him any good.

Sarah said <I hope he finds a good home.>

αSpike said <I am sure he will. Pedro never really belonged in this pack, anyway.>

Oskar said <I did not like Pedro.>

Fritzi said <You do not like anyone, Oskar.>

Oskar turned around and snapped at her. Oskar was like that. αSpike growled at Oskar, and Oskar put his tail between his legs.

One two three days later we lost Colleen. We had not expected to lose Colleen because she was an Irish setter, and big, although she was a dummy. She was too dumb to avoid being captured. After that, the pack stayed away from the outside world.

But in that same time we were joined by Nanook, a dumb Siberian husky; Rocky, a dumb Boxer female; and Neil, a smart St. Bernard. So the pack grew bigger.

I went back into the outside world by myself to see if αChris had returned. I went to our office, but my nose told me he had not been there in a long time. I went to our apartment. I went in and sniffed around, but he had not been there, either.

I stayed outside the door for one two three days. I only left to go out to piss and shit, and downstairs to the Nighthawk Diner to get some food. Whitey always fed me.

One day he said, "Where is Chris? I haven't seen him in a while."

I wished I could tell him, but I could not.

When I got back to the pack αSpike looked at me suspiciously. I could tell he was thinking about driving me out of the pack. Oskar's ears perked up. Oskar was always looking for trouble.

αSpike said <Where have you been?>

I lowered my head. I said <I went home to see if Chris had returned and was looking for me.>

αSpike said <And he had not?"

I said <No, he has not been there in many days.>

Nothing else was ever said about that.

———————

The map kept growing in my head. Every day we went looking and every day we came back to our den with nothing.

I noticed something about the map.

I said <Rin Tin Tin, there is something odd about the map.>

Rin Tin Tin said <Yes. There is a big hole in it.>

That was right. It was a hole. It was a very big hole. The hole was shaped like a hot dog.

(By that Sherlock meant it was a long, fat cylinder. Sherlock's analogies were often about food. I learned later that this particular hole—more like a void in the dogs' maps—was something like five miles long and a mile in diameter. It defined one parameter of Heinlein Town.—PC)

Rin Tin Tin said <Sherlock, every time we have gone close to the big hole we find a door that is shut. We cannot open them, and the only times we have seen these doors open, they are guarded by humans with guns.>

I said <Rin Tin Tin, how big is your map?>

Rin Tin Tin said <It is very big. Here, think about it and maybe I can show it to you.>

I did think about it, and saw at once that Rin Tin Tin's map was much larger than mine. Much, much, much larger. As I looked at the map, I saw that it was not just of Irontown, but of the larger world outside. I had much of this map inside my own head. I could see the path I had taken to αChris's mother's dinosaur farm. I could see many other places I had been.

Rin Tin Tin said <The map is even bigger than that. The map is in the outside place where my mind can go.>

I said <I know of this place. I can go there, too.>

Rin Tin Tin said <But I have much more of the map. Think with me and I will show you.>

I did think, and in my thinking the map in my head shrunk. It got smaller and smaller and I could see train lines linking different cities. I could not see details any longer. Then it kept shrinking. Then I saw that the map was curved, and it kept curving until it was a ball. I knew the ball had to be very, very large, but I could not understand just how large.

Then there was another ball, bigger than the first one. I have learned that this ball was known as Earth. The ball we were in was called Luna. Then the map got smaller and smaller until there was another little ball. I have learned that this ball was called Mars. There were more and more balls with names like Saturn and Neptune, Pluto and Charon.

Rin Tin Tin said <I think the empty space in my map is a ship.>

I said <I am not sure I know what a ship is.>

Rin Tin Tin said <It is like a train, but goes between these other balls. People ride in them.>

I did not really understand. I still do not really understand. I am a very smart dog, but this was too much for me. It was even too much for Spike, and he is a supersupersmart dog.

But the next day I went with the pack to one of the doors. We all sniffed around. Sarah put her nose right to the door, which was open just a little bit. We all noticed it when she came alert.

Sarah said <I smell something like what you said Chris smelled like.>

I went over and sniffed, and she was right. It did not just smell like αChris, it *was* αChris.

We moved the pack to a new den, where we could look at the door that led into the ship. I was so excited I could hardly eat. I knew that I would soon be seeing αChris.

The door was on a big open space that usually had a lot of people coming and going. There were trucks selling food and a place that sold ice cream. We begged some leftovers from some of the places. But we tried to keep out of sight as much as we could.

Not many people came and went through the door. When someone did, one of us would try to get close enough for a sniff. If the scent was close enough, I would walk over and get a closer look and sniff.

It was one two three days before he came out. I was asleep, and Fritzi woke me up. We looked across the open space, and I saw him. My heart leaped with joy. Then I saw that two humans were holding his arms and his hands were tied together. I felt the hair rising on the back of my neck. Fritzi was running around the plaza, gathering the pack. The pack came to me.

αSpike said <Is that him?>

I said <I am going to kill those humans.>

And I charged. I could hear the pack running behind me. I saw αChris was being taken to the ice-cream store. There were people sitting on chairs at tables and eating ice cream.

αChris turned, and I saw the look of joy spread across his face.

I recognized one of the humans who had taken αChris so long, long ago. I intended to rip his leg off this time.

I barked my fury at the men, and I leaped.

"Gretel," she said.

"Gretel," I said. I was about to say more—though I have no idea what that might have been—when she looked over my shoulder. Tom and the bruiser turned. I twisted out of their grips, and it could have been the perfect opportunity to escape, to run like hell . . . but what I saw was Sherlock, looking more like his wolf ancestors than I had ever seen him. He was followed by a pack of a couple dozen dogs.

Some of them were *big* dogs: a German shepherd, a Rottweiler, a Doberman. All had murder in their eyes.

"Sherlock!" I shouted. "Sherlock, stay!"

I had no idea if he would stop, but I knew that if these dogs actually attacked, no good could come of it. It would likely end up with one or both of us dead.

Besides, I really wanted to know why my old friend Gretel had kept me in a prison cell for so many weeks.

Sherlock faltered, and I thought the dogs behind him slowed a little, but I couldn't be sure.

"Sherlock! Sherlock! It's okay. I'm okay. They're going to let me go. Don't come any closer. Stay, Sherlock! Sit and stay!"

He stopped and shook his head, as if dazed. A Dalmatian, a beautiful dog, white with a thousand black spots, pulled up beside him. The rest of the pack circled nervously.

"Come here, Sherlock. I'm okay. Sit, old friend."

He sat.

I turned to Dick and held out my hands.

"If you know what's good for you, you'll uncuff me. I don't know how long I can keep him docile."

"Do as he says," Gretel said, behind me. I turned to look at her and saw a scary sight. There were at least seven or eight people back there behind her and beside her, and they all had guns that were leveled either at me or at the dogs.

I turned back and Tom opened the cuffs. I went down on one knee. I realized I was crying. I didn't need to say anything. Sherlock came to me and did something he never did.

He put his paws up on my shoulders and howled. Between howls, he licked my face. Dogs can't cry, they aren't equipped for it, but I knew that inside, Sherlock was weeping as much as I was.

"Is everyone okay?" Gretel asked. Between licks of my face, I squirmed around and saw the armed guards putting their weapons away.

"Good. Chris, can you introduce me to the famous Sherlock? We've been trying to catch him for weeks, but he's just too smart for us. His pack as well, who seem to be mostly CECs."

I was about to tell Sherlock to go over and meet her, but he was already trotting in that direction. He sniffed at the hand she held out to him, and then he howled. It was a different howl than the one when he came to me. It was a howl of triumph. He had found her.

"Mary Smith," I said.

"In the flesh. Hazel!"

A woman stuck her head out the door of the ice-cream parlor.

"Triple scoops of vanilla for all my canine friends here, if you please. On me."

The dogs ate ice cream until they were stuffed. Then most of them wandered away, but the Dalmatian stayed beside Sherlock. Gretel turned away from Sherlock and looked at me.

"I guess you will have some questions for me," she said.

"You might say that. It's not every day I get shanghaied onto a spaceship that isn't going anywhere."

"What is this shanghaied?"

"It's a nautical word for kidnapping."

She winced a little but nodded.

"Yeah, that's what we did."

"Well, the obvious question is . . . why? And the second one is what do you intend to do with me?"

"That's going to take a little while, but . . ."

Someone had come close to her and was trying to get her attention. She looked annoyed but stopped for a moment to consider something on a clipboard the woman was showing her. She nodded and signed her name, then waved the woman off. I noticed that there was a line of people behind her who all seemed to want her attention. What was going on here?

She stood up. I saw Sherlock and the Dalmatian come on the alert, watching us both closely.

"Everyone," she announced. "I'm taking an hour off. Go away, all of you. Come back later." She turned to me. "Come on. Let's get inside."

I followed her into the ice-cream parlor. Sherlock and the Dalmatian abandoned their ice-cream dishes and trotted right behind me. There was a woman behind the counter in the shop.

"What can I get you?" she asked. Gretel ordered pistachio almond fudge with chocolate syrup on top. Feeling more than a little disoriented, I said I'd have the same even though it sounded dreadful.

"Okay," said Gretel. "Why. The short answer is that we did it for your own protection. What are we going to do with you? You may have to go back to your room for a while, but you will be released soon."

"Cell," I said.

"Okay. Cell."

"Who are 'we'?"

She sighed. Hazel put dishes of ice cream in front of us. Gretel took a small spoonful of hers, and I decided to sample mine. I was surprised at how good it tasted.

"It's kind of hard to know where to begin."

"I've always thought the beginning is a good place."

"Yeah, but what's the beginning?"

"How about why did you hire me and Sherlock to find the guy who gave you a resistant form of leprosy against your will. Oh, excuse me, your hands seem to be okay."

She waved her hands in the air. "Yeah. That was just a temporary biohack. I cleared it up soon after I left your office. But that's not the beginning. That's closer to the end . . . though the real end is still a little way off . . . if all goes well."

She had sort of trailed off and gotten a faraway look in her eyes. For a moment, she looked much, much older than I knew her age to be.

"No, Chris, to get to the beginning, we have to go back a lot further than that. We have to go back to the day that you and I met.

"We have to go back to the Big Glitch."

You've heard of hearts skipping a beat? Mine ran a

hundred-meter dash and set a new Olympic record for the high jump.

"The thing is," she said, ". . . it's not over."

———————

"Since I saw you last," she said, "I've been on an emergency trip to Mars. I just got back. Otherwise, I would have looked at your case sooner."

"My case. What the hell does that mean?"

"I intended that you would track me down, then come with me, voluntarily, to Irontown. To Heinlein Town. We don't make much of a distinction these days. We're all in the same boat, so to speak."

"You mean the same ship."

"Yes, I suppose. You were quartered in a derelict space-ship called the *Robert A. Heinlein*. It was built to go to the stars, but it never left. It's been sitting here on the fringe of Irontown for over a century."

"There you go again. 'Quartered.'"

"All right, all right. I'm sorry . . . mostly. But it had to be done, and you'll see why in a moment."

"Don't you have more important things to do than explain things to me? You seem to be a very busy woman." There were lots of people waiting impatiently outside the shop.

"You have no idea." She got up and pulled a shade down over the window. "I really do have a thousand things I must do, but now at least we can have a little privacy. Aren't you going to eat your ice cream?" She took a spoonful of her own. "I'm usually eating on the run. Don't usually have time for dessert."

"Why does it sound to me like you're stalling? Is what you have to tell me really so bad?" I took another bite of my sundae.

"Mostly it depends on you. It is pretty bad, but there's hope, there's salvation, if you want to take it. Now, maybe we would do better if I just tell you the story. And then, if you have questions, I will answer them."

I made an "after you" gesture.

"You have the floor."

———

It was quite a tale she had to tell. And by the end of it my whole universe had been upended, set on its car. You probably have never had anyone tell you that everything you thought you knew about the world was wrong. Try it sometime. It will definitely get your motor running.

The main fact that I had to wrap my head around was that the years since the days of the Big Glitch had only been a pause, not an end.

"The remains of the CC are still out there," Gretel said. "Fragmented, contained, a shadow of his former self . . . but still out there."

"Sure," I said. "We have to have computers to run things. But they aren't AI, are they?"

"'Artificial Intelligence' has always been a slippery definition. A computer can sound sentient, but is it? Is it self-aware? Long ago computers began writing their own programs because humans just weren't capable of handling all the information needed. They sort of bootstrapped to the point where we were just before the Glitch. The CC had an individual personality tailored to millions of humans in Luna. Every living person viewed the CC as a close companion. Do you remember what that was like?"

"I think all of us do," I said. What I didn't mention was that, even after all the things the Central Computer had done to me . . . I still missed him. I missed that quiet voice in my head that knew me better than any human could.

"I don't remember, you see. Here in Irontown, we were always suspicious of the implanted tech that made mind-to-mind communication with the CC possible. I never got it. We had, and still have, a different system that we are sure we can dominate, rather than having it dominate us."

"And you were proved right."

"Yes. We get no pleasure from that. We suffered during the Glitch, just as much as the people outside our enclave did, just in a different way."

"Yeah. I was part of that suffering. I've always wished I could atone for that in some way."

"It's not necessary. I know how you were hoodwinked into the invading force. We understand that the CC did as much or more damage outside Irontown as you guys did to us inside."

In some ways, it was a miracle that so many of us survived. A million died when the systems the CC controlled stopped working or went haywire in other ways. We were saved by the fact that the CC was always a collective intelligence, and not all parts of it were involved in the attempted takeover of Irontown and the disasters that followed. In fact, parts of the CC remained sane and were probably the reason things kept working at all. They fought the rogue AI to a standstill.

Or so we were always told.

"That's more or less true," Gretel said. Then she made a back-and-forth gesture with one hand. "I don't pretend to understand it all. It's not my field. But the cyber-wonks around here say that the CC did fragment during the Glitch, as the result of a war between what we can think of as the 'good CC' and the 'bad CC,' the 'insane CC.' The CC that wanted to kill itself."

"But you said it's not over."

"No. We found out a long time ago that the CC had started to reassemble itself. We don't know much about the good CC, or if it's even out there. But the bad CC started growing less than a year after the Glitch. And it remembers everything. And it's crazier than ever.

"And it's pissed off."

———————

Well, that was a little hard to swallow. What was it doing? Just biding its time until the next Glitch?

245

"Something like that," she agreed. "But here's where you come in. The resurrected CC is operating just under the radar of the citizens outside. We can only observe it carefully, without alerting it to what we are doing. You can't imagine how hard that is. We have to do everything indirectly. We have to disguise all our actions as something else.

"See, I wanted to just invite you to come see me, but that was impossible. The thing is, you are being hunted, Chris."

"Hunted . . . How? Why?"

"Let's take the why first. The CC has been in contact again with the Charonese Mafia. The CC doesn't really give a damn about you, but it's willing to do the detective work the Charonese need to track down the individuals they are after."

"And I'm one of them?"

"All of you ex-Invaders are." She paused. "That's what we call you in here, both cops and Charonese mercenaries. Invaders."

"I can't protest. That's what we did."

"I don't know what you know about the Charonese Mafia."

"Very little, I guess. I know they are ruthless. You saw yourself when they went around killing all the survivors of the Invasion. By the way, I never got a chance to thank you properly for saving my life."

"You saved mine first."

I shrugged.

"That was nothing to what you did. So thank you."

She gave me a twisted little smile.

"You cursed me for putting you through all that pain."

"I don't remember that."

"You were delirious. I didn't take it seriously."

We looked at each other for a moment over the remains of our ice-cream sundaes. I heard Sherlock stir and get to his feet. He rested his head on my thigh. I knew he could sense that something was up. I knew it, too, but I didn't know what it was.

"The main thing you should know about the Charonese Mafia is that they never forget, they never forgive, and they never give up."

"That sounds like a lethal combination," I observed.

"You better believe it. And it concerns you. They've been hunting you for at least ten years that I know of. They intend to kill you."

———————

"It's not like the Charonese have a regiment of assassins in Luna looking for you. We think it's only two, maybe three. And they find it difficult to move about because they are here illegally, and they probably have warrants out for them from the invasion."

"Ugly and Uglier," I muttered.

"What?"

"Never mind. Go on."

"We think you are one of the last ones left. Maybe *the*

last one. You pointed out that I saw them executing the survivors during the invasion. They intend to finish the job, no matter how long it takes."

"But why? Do they think I might testify against them?"

"That may have been how this custom of theirs started. Leave no witnesses. It's a gangster trademark going back centuries, back to criminal groups on Old Earth. It seems that now it's just a tradition. But they are very, very big on traditions. It's a major part of their culture, if you want to dignify their society as a culture."

And now they were after me.

————————

"The biggest thing that has kept you alive is your lack of cyber implants," Gretel said. "The Charonese had no good way to identify you. The revived CC was no help, partly because we have been fighting it for years with cyber attacks. See, this new consciousness is even more frightening, in some ways, than the old one. It is capricious, paranoid, elusive. It hides from us and plots our deaths, but we have managed to keep it confused. But that's getting less and less effective. It's growing, and getting smarter and bolder. It's been a shell game for years, with the Heinleiners working games on the CC, but he's catching on. He's getting better at guessing which of the several sextillion moving cups the little pea is hiding under. Which puts us all in danger.

"You were a special case, though. At least to me. As you might have noticed, I'm sort of a leader around here. My father is the real leader, but he's too busy with other things to take charge, and besides, he's too wrapped up in his science. He's not that great in social situations."

"Would that be V. M. Smith?" I asked.

For the first time, she looked surprised.

"How did you know that?" she asked, suspiciously.

"I read Hildy Johnson's book. She said she was going to the stars. On a ship called the *Heinlein*. I put two and two together. You're Smith's crazy daughter, right?"

She smiled.

"I'll accept that title. So, yeah, that's my dad. He's still . . . tinkering with his 'hyperdrive.' That's what he calls it, anyway. Supposed to get us to Alpha Centauri in a few days." Without actually scoffing, she managed to imply to me that she was not holding her breath waiting for that to happen.

Why anyone would want to go to Alpha was a good question. Our probes had reported back that none of the planets there were any more suitable for life than Luna was. So why put all that effort into going there, just to start making more burrows in the rock?

But I supposed she meant that the hyperdrive would open up the stars to us. If it could go four light-years in a few days, just about anything in the galaxy was within reach.

"We found out that one or both of the Charonese assassins here in Luna had gotten a line on your whereabouts.

Probably from the CC. I decided that we had to pull you in."

"Yeah. Pull me in. Put me in a cell for several weeks."

"Again, I'm sorry about that. But like I said, I had to be on Mars, and I'm the only one who can interrogate you."

"That's what this is? An interrogation."

"I'm trying to determine what we should do with you."

"Why not just send me home? I'll take my chances with the Charonese. So why not let me go?"

"Sorry, that's the one thing I can't do. At least, not yet. No matter how this turns out, you won't be going back to your apartment for a while. You'll be staying here."

I felt I had been calm and reasonable ever since being taken from my cell. But it *was* a cell, I *was* a prisoner, and I had finally had enough of playing nice with everybody. I stood up, angrily. Both Sherlock and the Dalmatian got to their feet, on alert.

"Dammit, you said you were going to explain all this to me. You've been dancing around something. Why don't you just come out and say it?"

She was unfazed by my anger. She looked at me calmly.

"What I'm trying to determine," she said, "is whether you go back into your cell or become a free citizen of Irontown. There is no third choice.

"Bottom line. Can we trust you?"

twenty _____

SHERLOCK

like vanilla ice cream. I also like tutti-frutti ice cream. I also like strawberry, peach, butter pecan, apricot, fig, and papaya ice cream. These are the flavors of the Cosmic Catastrophe Big Glitch Sundae that Hazel makes in her ice-cream parlor. There are eight flavors in the Cosmic Catastrophe Big Glitch Sundae. I once ate a Cosmic Catastrophe Big Glitch Sundae. It had eight scoops. I ate eight, get it? Ha-ha.

But I was not eating a Cosmic Catastrophe Big Glitch Sundae on the day when we found αChris and αChris was taken to see Mary Smith, AKA Delphine RR Blue Suede Shoes. AKA is a word we private detectives use. It means Also Known As.

On that day I had eaten three scoops of vanilla ice

cream. I think vanilla is my favorite flavor of ice cream. Though I also like butter pecan and strawberry. Spike was beside me, nodding off. I did not call him αSpike anymore because αChris was now my only alpha. This made me happy.

(And I must cut you off there, feeling happy, Sherlock. You will get to speak again, I promise, but since I have been given the role of amanuensis, historian, and editor of this strange tale [or tail, if you will, ha-ha!] more or less by default, I must let Chris continue to have the floor, to preserve some sort of continuity. He still has more to tell of his reunion with Gretel.——PC)

CHRIS

"There's a lot going on here that I don't understand," I said. "At least, it seems to me that all that incredibly complicated business of the para-leprosy—which didn't exist—and the trail through the Chinese restaurant, all that bullshit, that was all just a scam, you were actually *leading* me to that empty apartment . . . but why? Why didn't you just invite me? I would have come, you know that. Then you locked me up. Why didn't you—"

"I'm really pressed for time, Chris. Let me go on for a minute or two, okay?

"Remember I told you about the shell game we're playing? We shuffle and jive, we spoof and we fake, we hoax and we counterfeit. We cover up everything. If I had gone straight to you and asked you to join us here in Irontown, the CC would have seen it, and you would likely be dead by now. Me, too, probably. So we have to keep that little pea moving.

"We have created blank spots in the cyber world. We move things in and out of them. I wanted you here, but I didn't dare approach you. That apartment doesn't exist in any database. In fact, that whole corridor is a ghost. Nobody lives there, but we maintain records showing that they do. We gassed you and took you down a stairway that doesn't exist, and along a corridor linking Irontown to the outer world that also does not exist.

"Before that, I left a trail for you to follow. The whole ruse with the leprosy. I thought that would get your attention. The business of me working at the Chinese restaurant. I was only there long enough to leave a scent trail for Sherlock. Pumpkin lied about knowing me. She's one of us, one of the people who work what we call the Underground Railway. She's a lot smarter than she acts, by the way. In fact, she's one of our best cyber-wonks. She was the one who wrote that whole scenario

"There is also another problem. There are those . . . well, let's just say that not all Heinleiners wanted you here. There is still resentment over the invasion, and you were on the other side, don't forget."

". . . I don't know how to say I'm sorry for something as awful as that."

"Don't worry about it. As the boss, I can do a lot of stuff, but I'm not all-powerful. In the end, a compromise was reached. We decided that if you were good enough, *smart* enough, to follow me to the apartment, well, then you could have an invitation. If you couldn't find me, you would never be the wiser, and you would be on your own."

"An invitation to what?"

She drew herself up, looked into my eyes, took a deep breath, and finally got around to it.

"We're going to the stars, and you are invited."

"What . . . you mean Alpha Centauri in a few days?"

She smiled.

"No. That was an exaggeration. And it's not really a 'hyperdrive,' in the sense of going into hyperspace, whatever that is, or through a wormhole, or a black hole, whatever those are. I don't understand it, but it's something new my father invented. It works, it doesn't use rocket engines, and it is very, very fast. Alpha Centauri in . . . about ten years, ship's time."

"But there's nothing—"

"No, we're not going to Alpha, you're right, there's nothing there that's worth the trip. That was just an example. The star we're heading for is more like forty light-years away. There are two Earth-like planets in that system. We're hoping at least one of them is habitable and doesn't have people, or intelligent beings, anyway, already living there. If neither is suitable, we move on to the next star."

The idea of getting on a ship and heading out to Betelgeuse or some damn place like that was alarming, but there was something else that somehow took precedence in my mind. I found it hard to express. But it had to be said.

"So everything I did to find you, all the tracking I did . . . well, actually, Sherlock did, mostly . . . that was all you leading me around by the nose. All that time, you were playing me for a sap."

"I don't know what a sap is."

"Old pulp-fiction slang for a clueless idiot."

"Okay, you could say that—"

"I don't know how else you could put it."

She looked a little angry at that.

"How about I was working very hard to save your ass?"

"I didn't ask for it. I don't think I want it. Why would I want to get on your crazy starship, which will probably blow up halfway to Neptune? I've got a life here."

She didn't say anything. She didn't *have* to say anything. I felt my face getting hot. Sure, Chris, you've got a life, pretending to be a film-noir shamus from the twentieth century. Sitting on my ass in my retro office and waiting for clients to come in the door. And how many clients have you had in the last few years, Chris? Well, it wouldn't take long to count the custom-made manila folders in my big metal file cabinet.

Sure, you've got a life. A pretend life. A make-believe life.

But it was my life, and I intended to go on living it.

"One more question," I said. "Why me? Of all the millions of people who don't live in this crazy Irontown, why me? You think you will desperately need a private detective in interstellar space?"

"Actually, we *are* trying to take at least one of every skill, every profession, because if we need one, it won't be possible to go back.

"But that's not the main reason, Chris. You could say that I have an investment in you. I spent a lot of time keeping you alive, and I can't bear to think a Charonese assassin is going to come along and murder you. So it's personal."

"Gretel, I have about as much faith in these Charonese assassins and this coming Big Glitch Part Two as I have in your dad's hyperdrive."

"Well, you don't have to believe me. You have the option of staying behind. Maybe you're right. Maybe we will blow up on takeoff, and maybe the killers will never find you. But the Second Big Glitch? That's real. I have spent the last five years of my life battling to keep it from happening. And I'm losing. We are all losing."

"I think I'll stay behind, then, and thank you very much for the invitation and the unexpected stay in your little hotel. So, can I go?"

She grimaced.

"I'm afraid not. See, you know too much now. You can't go back home until just before the ship takes off."

"And how long is that? You have a timetable?"

"No. No set date. But it will have to be soon."

"Terrific. So I guess the gorilla will take me back to my cell now."

"Soon." She leaned forward. "Chris, I wish you would think about it some more. Everything I've told you is very real. The ship is being readied and provisioned and stocked with everything we think we could possibly need at our destination. And if you think getting you here was insanely complicated, just think how hard it has been keeping all that work, all those preparations, secret from the CC."

"I guess so. It hardly matters to me, though. I'm going back into the can. Stir. The slammer, the hoosegow, the calaboose."

"I'm sorry, Chris. I really am. I had so hoped that you would go with us." She looked down, then into my eyes. "See, there is one more reason I wanted to rescue you. Like I said, it's personal. During that awful time, I . . . well, I developed quite a crush on you."

Her face was actually red. I had no idea how to respond to that. I was still getting used to the idea of Gretel, little heroic Gretel, as a grown woman. Now I looked at her, and saw her as an adult for the first time. I could see the ten-year-old I had known and the woman she had become.

And I didn't want to think about it. I'd think about it in my cell tomorrow. Because tomorrow is another day.

"I do want to know one more thing, though. Where is this ship?"

She laughed out loud.

"You've been living in it."

"But . . ." That didn't seem possible. Not that I had been in a ship, I knew that. But I hadn't realized it was *the* ship.

The *Heinlein* was a derelict on a grand scale. Pretty much everyone who had been paying attention at all to the history of the last hundred years knew it was out there, a giant beached steel whale, rumored to be five miles long. In reality, who knew? Because you could hardly see it. For a hundred years the crater where it lay had been used as a dumping ground for all the junk of three cities. In fact, the Heinleiners had used this junk when they built their separate city.

For many decades, no one thought it would ever rise again. Hell, right then, I didn't believe it would ever fly. It was not as if they had just heaped the rubbish against the sides of the ship, to be shaken off when it rose on . . . what? The hyperdrive? The ship had been *built right into* Irontown. From where I was sitting, I could see a small piece of its massive hull, and the attachments were far more than just a clothesline strung from an apartment to an anchor point on the ship.

No, stuff was welded to the ship. Apartments clung like barnacles to the metal. There was trash surrounding it, attached to it. There was no way in the world that the *Heinlein* would ever shake free of all that.

I mentioned some of this to Gretel.

"That's exactly what we want the CC to think," she said, placidly. "We have built a dummy ship five hundred miles from here, and there's where the CC has been looking. If we keep it looking there just a little while longer, we should be okay.

"And I'm sorry, but I have to go now. Please don't fight it, Chris. Tom will take you—"

I never got to hear the end of that sentence because a

huge blast blew her across the room and against Hazel's service counter.

SHERLOCK

I was dreaming. I was half-asleep, but I can dream when I am only half-asleep. I was with αChris, and I was happy. He was throwing a ball, and I was running after it. Then there were rabbits. I do not know where the rabbits came from, but there were rabbits. I was chasing one of the rabbits. I have never chased a rabbit, but I have often dreamed of that.

I was with αChris and I was very happy in the dream. I opened one eye and looked up. There was αChris. I had lost αChris for a while, but I had looked for him, and I had found him. Everything was all right in the world.

Chris was talking to the woman named Gretel. Gretel had petted my head and scratched behind my ears when we were introduced. I liked Gretel. I did not hear what they were saying to each other.

I was on the floor next to Spike. We both had bellies full of Hazel's vanilla ice cream. Spike was twitching in his sleep, so I knew he was dreaming, too. I wondered if he was chasing rabbits in his dream. I wondered if I could join him in his dream. I do not know where I go when I dream, so maybe we could both be in the same dream. I would like that.

There was a very loud noise. I do not like very loud noises. This was the loudest noise I have ever heard. I have learned that the very loud noise was caused by a bomb. The bomb was thrown from a special gun that throws bombs. As soon as it exploded there were more bomb explosions from outside the ice-cream parlor, but these were not so close.

The closest bomb had blown out the window of the ice-cream parlor. Spike and I were on the ground, and the broken glass passed over our heads. But some of the pieces of glass had fallen on me and Spike. There was also a lot of dust on me. I leaped to my feet. I shook off the dust and glass. I was very scared.

αChris was shouting, "Gretel! Gretel!"

There was more shouting outside. I did not know where to turn. I saw Spike. I had thought the flying glass did not hit him, but I was wrong. There were some big pieces of glass in his side and in the side of his head. He did not get up.

I saw αChris kneeling down beside Gretel. Gretel was not moving. There was a lot of blood. I smelled many things, too many things to sort out. I have learned that some of the things I smelled were from the exploding bomb. I have learned that that is what gunpowder smells like when it burns.

I nudged Spike with my nose, and then pawed at him. He whined and tried to sit up. He could not sit up. One of his eyes was gone. I howled.

But I could not be afraid. I had to be strong. I heard people outside running toward the ice-cream parlor. I had never smelled people who smelled like that before. I have learned that the smell was the sweat of humans called

Charonese. These Charonese humans liked to fight. When they decided to fight, they took a drug that made them stronger. They took another drug that made them not afraid. They took another drug that made pain go away. All these drugs came out in their sweat and in their piss.

Charonese are bad humans. I do not like Charonese humans.

I could hear them coming. I could smell them coming. I went to the door of the ice-cream parlor and looked out. I saw many humans lying on the ground. Some of them were moving. Some of them were screaming. Some of them were not moving. Some of them were in pieces.

There were two large humans coming toward the ice cream parlor. I knew these were the Charonese humans who smelled so different.

I wanted to run away. But αChris was behind me. I must protect αChris.

I must become a wolf.

I felt the rage boiling up inside my heart. I would be strong, and I would be brave.

I would kill. I would kill and kill and kill.

CHRIS

The bomb went off about thirty yards from where we were sitting. Sometimes your life is determined by a roll of the dice. I had been sitting in a chair with a wall to my left. The force of the blast buckled the wall, but did not blow it down.

Another roll of the dice determined that Gretel was sitting facing me over the table, with a big glass window to her right. The blast shattered the window and picked her up, along with her chair and the table, and threw them across the room.

The fact that I had been shielded didn't mean I was unharmed, but I didn't know about my injuries until later. They were minor compared to the devastation visited on Gretel. Some of the shards of glass slashed at my arm and the side of my face.

Worse than the minor injuries was the sense of disorientation. I was not concussed, but I was damn close to it. I was deafened, unable to hear anything but a very loud ringing in my ears. I found myself on my hands and knees. I looked up and saw the Dalmatian that had come with Sherlock. He was on his side, pretty torn up, not moving. I couldn't tell if he was breathing. I looked around, but I didn't see Sherlock.

What I did see was Gretel, crumpled up, twisted, flayed open from scalp to waist. I got to my feet and staggered over to her.

I was amazed to see she was conscious. Her right cheek was ripped open. One of her eyes was wounded, and I'm sure she was as deaf as me, but she was moving, trying to get to her feet.

The ringing in my ears was still loud, but I was beginning to hear other sounds. Somewhere water was jetting and splashing, probably from a broken pipe. There was a loud hissing sound.

Was that gunfire I heard?

"Help, help, help me . . ." She slurred her words. It was a wonder she could talk at all. "What happened?"

"I don't know," I said. "An explosion. A bomb?"

"Are we being attacked?" She tried even harder to get up, seemingly unaware that her right arm was almost ripped off, and both of her legs were twisted in ways they aren't supposed to twist. I could see bone poking through her pants.

"I don't know, Gretel. You need to calm down. I'm sure help is on the way." The only good news I could see was that no arteries seemed to be opened. She was oozing and dripping blood all over, but it wasn't spurting.

As to the help . . . I said it was coming to try to calm her down, but now I wondered. I was sure I heard gunfire. I was unarmed. It seemed the best idea was to lie low until I had a better idea of what was happening.

But it was getting noisier out there. I decided I'd better get up and try to find out what was going on.

"You just lie quietly," I told Gretel. Her eye wasn't tracking all that well, and I thought she might be beginning to feel the pain. I wondered if she was going into shock. I didn't know what the symptoms were. Hell, I barely even knew any basic first aid. Hoping I was right in leaving her for a moment, I cautiously got to my feet and, keeping my head low, went to the remains of the window.

It was a mess outside. It was all too reminiscent of the day of the Big Glitch. It was like I was reliving it, and that was the last thing in the entire universe I wanted to do.

Wreckage was strewn for quite a distance from Hazel's parlor. Most of it was off to my left, though, so I thought it was possible the bomb had not been thrown directly at us. It was much worse over there. I couldn't remember what had been there, and there wasn't much left to tell me what it had been. Another several storefronts, I thought.

There were bodies everywhere.

Just outside the parlor, they were heaped in a horrific tumble of torn limbs and blood. No one over there was moving. I remembered that those had been Gretel's lieutenants, the dozen or so people who had been waiting impatiently for her to get through with me so she could get back to the important business of organizing the final preparations for the departure of the *Heinlein*. None of them would be organizing anything now.

Elsewhere I saw people crawling. A few had made it to their feet and were staggering around. None of them seemed to be very aware of where they were going. Some were horribly maimed and burned.

I wondered again if Gretel had been the target, or had it been just a bit of bad luck for us, or good luck for them, that she had been hit.

Once more, I saw that in the heat of battle it can be impossible to tell what is going on.

I saw people beginning to move in from the edges of the

destruction. Were they on our side, on Gretel's side? Or were they attackers? It was important to know, because I had a growing certainty that this was part of the continuation of the Big Glitch Gretel had spoken of. In which case, the invaders would not be friendly forces.

Some of the people were clearly trying to render aid to the injured, but that didn't last long. I saw one would-be rescuer go down in a spray of blood, then another, and then everyone was taking cover as gunfire began peppering the open area. So I had an idea where the enemy was.

From the other side of the plaza, the side where I knew the *Heinlein* was, a few people had begun to return fire. For the moment, none of the fighters from either side were showing themselves. So again, I decided the best course was to keep my head down and try to shield Gretel from what was still going on outside.

Because after all she had gone through, all we had both gone through, I was not about to lose her. Come what may, I was going to be by her side.

———

Looking back, it couldn't have been more than a few minutes, but it seemed like much longer. I spent most of that time trying to keep Gretel from attempting to rise. She was stubborn, she was a leader, and she was determined not to just lie there.

I ducked my head around the corner again when it seemed like there was a lull in the fighting. No one was moving in the devastated open area, but I could see muzzle flashes now and then coming from what I thought was the enemy side of the plaza. It didn't look like a good idea to try to get out of the parlor. So I checked the back, hoping there would be a service entrance leading deeper into the mazes of Irontown. I figured anything would be better than being pinned down here.

There probably was a back entrance, but the explosion had piled so much tangled wreckage that I couldn't budge any of it. I could see the door back there, but the frame seemed to be warped, so even if I could reach it, there was a good chance I wouldn't be able to get through to whatever was on the other side. I was frustrated and came back to Gretel, who at least had stopped struggling.

All this time I had hardly been aware of Sherlock. When I did notice him he seemed to be sticking close to my heels. Probably terrified, I thought, and who could blame him?

Suddenly a horn began to blare. It was very loud, a rising and falling tone interrupted by an earsplitting on-and-off buzzer, then a horrible hooting sound that seemed to split my skull. Sherlock began to howl. I can't imagine how painful it must have been to his sensitive ears.

My wrist was seized in a grip that I thought might break my bones. It was Gretel, grabbing me with the strength of hysteria. But when I put my head down to hear what she wanted to say, she was eerily calm. One side of her face was a horror mask, but her one good eye bored into me.

"Emer . . . emerg . . . emerge . . ."

"Emergency?"

She nodded, quickly.

"T . . . t . . ." She shook her head in frustration, then made a strange gesture with her good hand. Palm down, she swooped it through an arc until the fingers were pointing up. I didn't get it. She did it again.

"Emergency . . . emergency . . . you're kidding me. Takeoff?"

She nodded, her good eye boring into me.

"You can't do that! The ship is still hooked up into town, isn't it?"

She nodded again.

"How soon?"

She spread her fingers. Twice.

"Ten minutes?" She nodded. "Gretel, we're all going to die."

She shook her head.

"Not ffff . . . not fuh . . . not if—"

"Not if we hurry?"

She nodded.

"What do I do?"

She made a lifting gesture.

"Gretel, that's going to hurt like hell."

"Do it . . . no choice."

I sighed and got my arms under her. I was afraid her arm was going to fall off.

She never made a sound. I went through the door and out into the plaza. If things had been confused before, it was pandemonium now. People were emerging from hiding, clearly worried about getting shot, but even more afraid of being in Irontown when the *Heinlein* took off. *If* it took off, I added to myself. But if it exploded, or even if it just sat there on the ground, it was clear that all connections to this area and all the other areas around the ship were going to be severed. If I were doing that, I'd probably use explosives. Far away, back toward civilization, pressure doors would automatically shut, sealing those of us who didn't make it to the ship inside what would soon become a death chamber.

"Which way?" I asked. Gretel managed to nod toward my right. I started off in that direction, Sherlock trotting along at my heels. There was still shooting going on, and I couldn't do a damn thing about that. I had to hope that the attackers were as confused and disoriented as I was.

A bullet went sizzling by so close I could hear it. I picked up my pace. A moving target is harder to hit than a stationary one. Isn't it?

Most of the folks I could see were heading in the same direction. I hoped they all knew where they were going. I hurried along a wide connecting corridor, and at least the gunfire stopped for a few minutes. But I came out in another plaza, about the same size as the first one, and there was fighting there, too. Ahead of me a man was struck with a bullet. He went down, and I almost stumbled over him. I looked down and saw him clutching his thigh, which was spurting blood. I wanted to help him, but there was no way

I could manage to do that and still carry Gretel. I chanced a look back after I'd gone a few yards and saw someone grab his arm and yank him to his feet.

Down yet another wide corridor, then out into the largest open space I had yet seen in Irontown. Off to my right was a smooth surface that I hoped was the outer hull of the *Heinlein*. I tried to remember just what the ship looked like from the pictures I had found after the Big Glitch. What I recalled was a series of shapes with no obvious pattern to them. Cylinders, spheres, irregular trapezoids. A fair amount of ports and larger windows. Nothing I could see looked familiar, except for what was clearly an extralarge cargo lock. Boxes and pallets were scattered around the lock. I guessed it was cargo that was yet to be loaded. I hoped there was nothing absolutely critical in the containers because there was no chance at all that most of them would ever make it aboard.

Still, some of them must have been pretty important, as stevedore robots were hard at work lifting the boxes and carrying them toward the lock, supervised by frantic men and women in yellow coveralls.

"Yellow uniforms, cargo handlers," Gretel told me. "Blue . . . crew."

"Blue crew?"

"Blue uniforms. Crew. Know where to go."

"We have to get there first."

"Get us inside. Hurry."

The lock was drawing people like a big magnet. People in

all manner of dress were funneling toward it, some of them pausing to turn around and get off a shot or two, others trying to shield small children. Off in the other direction, invaders must have been converging because I could hear more gunfire coming from there and I saw another person go down.

The crowd was inevitably compressed as it neared the lock. This made them easier targets. But off to each side and from vantages higher up on the hull, people in red uniforms were returning intense fire toward the invaders. I could hear it even over the racket of the multiple klaxon horns.

"Almost there," I breathed to Gretel. I looked back. I couldn't see Sherlock. I shouted his name.

I had to save Gretel. I had to save Sherlock. What to do?

I decided I would get Gretel to the lock and give her to somebody, then go back for my dog.

Something caused me to turn. A sixth sense? I could not possibly have heard anything. For some reason I turned a full one-eighty, and saw a two-legged rhinoceros headed right for me.

Okay, he wasn't quite that big, but he was at least double my size. He was part of a line of charging pachyderms, and I didn't have to take too many guesses to figure out where he was from.

There is a certain sameness to Charonese, or at least to warriors, which is all I have ever seen. Maybe they have little guys and gals back home, where the babbling brooks of liquid nitrogen meander through the summer landscape. Or maybe not. They're not telling.

Half his head was blown off, and he was still coming. Whatever had hit him had just peeled back the skin from the entire right side of his face, exposing his steel skull, taking a lot of his cheekbone and lips with it. One eye was torn out. The skull replacement helps them survive injuries that otherwise would certainly be fatal.

But what no steel plate can protect you against is concussion. Whatever hit him had rattled around whatever he used for brains inside that silvery skull. He was staggering, looking quite confused. I could see a deep dent the bullet had made in the steel. He was just part of a line that was advancing steadily. They were taking casualties, but they just kept coming.

I was directly in the line of sight of his one good eye, which slowly began tracking. He pointed a pistol at me. It was an old-fashioned automatic, from a design hundreds of years old. I figured I was dead. He pulled the trigger. It clicked. It clicked again, and again. Cursing, he dropped the gun and lunged the last few feet between us. Before I knew it, he was on me.

I dropped Gretel. For the first time, she cried out. I probably did, too, as fingers like grappling hooks bit into my shoulder. He pulled his fist back for a punch that would have taken my head off.

That's when Sherlock came flying through the air like a guided missile and bit down on his forearm, hard. I could hear bones crack. At that moment other loud sounds began to be heard. It was a series of explosions, distant, but getting louder with each big bang. I realized it was the sound of the *Heinlein* being blasted free of all its encrustations.

But I had an even more immediate problem, which was to somehow keep the warrior from tearing my shoulder from its socket. And an even bigger problem was to keep the son of a bitch from killing Sherlock.

It's a good thing he was concussed. He reached toward me with his free hand, then realized it wasn't free, that there was a rather large dog clinging to that arm. So he turned his attention to Sherlock, and I did my best to use my only useful thumb to put out his other eye. Blinded, he went after me in a rage, grunting like a pig. And Sherlock was there again, not letting go except to get a better grip.

We only had minutes. Maybe even less than a minute. The explosions were very loud now. They were set to explode in a series, and each one was closer to us. There was the loudest bang of all, and with a screech of tortured metal, the ship began to come free. The warrior and I both looked up, and I could see the side of the ship coming free of all the things that had been attached to it. Walls tore open. Things spilled out. A gap began to grow. And a high wind began to howl. Clouds of condensation formed and swirled like some awful fog from Hell.

The air was going. With it went small objects, sucked right up and out through the gap. Eventually, we would all be lifted. Me, Sherlock, the Charonese, and the Dalmatian.

The Dalmatian? Where had he come from?

Injured as he was, he managed to get into the fight, grabbing the killer by the ankle and pulling. The killer tumbled to the ground, taking me with him. And then there were even more dogs on him. For a moment I couldn't even see him for the snarling, twisting, tearing mass of dogs.

Pieces were coming off the Charonese. Mostly it was bits of his clothes and equipment belt, but some of it was chunks of flesh. I hoped they would strip him to the bone.

I realized that the hard object under me was the gun he had dropped. On his belt I saw a full clip of bullets. I managed to get it without getting my hand ripped off by the dogs. And now my addiction to violent movies from the past came in handy.

I knew how to release the empty clip. I knew how to jam the full clip into the butt. I knew how to jack a round into the chamber. I jammed the pistol against his lips. He cried out, giving me just enough room to slip the muzzle inside his mouth.

I pulled the trigger, sending a bullet through the soft, unprotected roof of his mouth. The metal cranium was tough. The bullet did not go through it. I could only imagine the bullet bouncing around in there. Smoke came out of his mouth, nose, and ears. He went instantly and totally limp.

I got to my feet. The wind was really shrieking now. I could feel it, a steady blast against my back, blowing toward the ship.

I saw the air lock begin to crank closed.

"Sherlock, let go!" I shouted. "Come on, boy!"

I actually had to kick him. He let go and looked at me in shock.

"To the ship!" I yelled. He began to bark, but he trotted along beside me as I picked up Gretel and staggered toward the ship.

The dogs were faster. All but the Dalmatian ran past me. Sherlock lingered with me.

People were still getting through the closing air lock. The gap between the ship and where I stood was five feet, and getting wider. Guards were looking at us all suspiciously. They didn't want strangers, like me, to get inside. The wind wasn't whistling quite as loudly now. The air was very thin. I would soon pass out. But I was still able to shout.

"This is Gretel, you guys!"

I must have been heard because when I jumped the gap, they let me in. I worried that they would not admit Sherlock, but they did. Already inside were about a dozen other dogs, all of them with blood around their mouths. I think the guards had seen them take down the Charonese.

The lock clanked closed behind us, and I heard the welcome air hissing into the lock.

———————

I kept waiting for the ship to blow up. But it didn't. Whatever driving power "Mr. Smith" had invented was getting us up and away quite smartly.

Naturally it was chaotic for a while there in the lock and

the spaces beyond. Gretel was not the only one badly injured. There were several dead people, and at least one who died right there in the lock before help could get to him. Gretel was recognized and whisked away, and soon the other casualties were either being treated or taken to medical facilities.

I didn't have much to do but sit there and try to catch my breath. There were several big screens on the walls, and I watched numbly as a hundred cameras both from the surface and aboard ship relayed the pictures to us. I saw the massive ship rising from the sea of trash like some iron whale breaching . . . but this whale never splashed back down. I saw the view looking down on the huge hole where Irontown had been. Debris was spewing into the vacuum, strewing itself over the ancient Lunar plain.

Many people died that day, but no one from beyond Irontown. The Heinleiners had been scrupulous in shutting the air locks that led to the city.

Sherlock rested his head in my lap. Someone had borne away the Dalmatian. I didn't know if he was dead or alive. The other dogs stuck close to me. I wondered what that was about.

Sherlock and I were pretty far down the triage list, but eventually a medic got to us. He saw to my wounds and gave me something for the pain. He even called in a vet for Sherlock.

In time someone asked me where I was to be billeted, and I told her I didn't know, that I wasn't on the passenger manifest. She gave me a cabin number, and I found my way to it in the massive maze of the ship. It turned out to be a barracks very much like the one where I had been held captive for all that time. I was too bone weary to laugh at that.

I threw myself down on the nearest bunk and slept like the dead.

epilog _____

wasn't shanghaied into a trip to the stars. In the end, I went voluntarily.

There were several opportunities to get off if I had still wanted to. The captain didn't give the *Heinlein* full power at the very start. We cruised into a fast orbit for Mars, but before that we lingered in the area as three much smaller ships docked with us, carrying people who had actually booked passage but happened to be elsewhere when the hammer fell. Two of those ships were quickly attached to the hull of the *Heinlein*. They would be modified into atmosphere landers if we . . . *when* we found an Earth-like planet. The other ship was made available to anyone who had been unintentionally stranded aboard the ship, or who had gotten cold feet about setting off into the interstellar void. I thought about it . . .

. . . but what did I have to go back to in Luna? My

mother would barely miss me, and I had no other family. I'd send her a postcard now and then until we got a few light-years out.

My job? Don't make me laugh. Somewhere along the line when I was being shot at by Charonese gangsters, I admitted to myself that being a private eye was really little more than a hobby. I could continue the hobby on my way to the stars.

There was also the fact that I *was* being shot at. I had been dubious about Gretel's claims of a continuation of the Big Glitch. Now I wasn't so sure. If things were going to get worse with the CC, I had no great desire to stick around and see it.

Come to think of it, I would write Mom and tell her she had better get herself to Mars or Mercury or some other place not ruled by the CC. Would she believe me? Possibly. Would she leave her precious breeding stock? Doubtful.

Were Mars and Mercury and points outward really going to be safe havens? Not even Gretel could say with any certainty.

———

We rendezvoused with ships from Mars, then from Ceres. Both had smaller colonies of Heinleiners. The ships carried those Martians and Cereans who wanted to go, and a lot of last-minute supplies.

As Gretel had said, there had been those who were extremely dubious of her desire to take me, an ex-Invader, on the ship. Most of those dissenters were won over by my "heroics" in rescuing Gretel. I even had several come up to me and admit that they had been against me, then give me a hearty slap on the back to show they had changed their minds.

———————

As for the Charonese . . . no one doubted that they would have shot us out of the sky if they could. No one knew for sure just what sort of nastiness they could send after us in the way of guided missiles. There just wasn't much information about that. But no one would have been surprised if they had some quite sophisticated space weapons, probably involving nuclear warheads.

But it was academic. Pluto and Charon were on the other side of the solar system from our path to the Goldilocks Star, which is what we were calling it rather than its astronomical catalog number. There was no way they could have reached us.

———————

Then there is the matter of Sherlock. I don't think I've ever been so frustrated.

On the one hand, if I hadn't been one of the weirdos who didn't have any cyber implants, it is certain that I would have been found and killed. Only my being off the grid saved my life. It was all pure bull-headedness on my part, and yet it turned out to be one of the wisest decisions I had ever made.

On the other hand, by not being cyber-ready, I missed all those years of a closer relationship with my dog.

My dog? No, I'll never look at him that way again. I now have implants that hook me into the ultramonitored, ultra-secure shipboard cyber-system. I was reluctant to do that, as my fear of having something in my head was still there, but I got over it.

And the first thing that happened was I was able to tune in to Sherlock's thoughts and emotions. Not all at once. You have to train for that; no one is born to be a dog whisperer. But I'm working at it. Right now I can only feel his biggest, most surface thoughts, and they don't express themselves in words. But I have learned much already.

I knew we were close, I knew I loved him and he loved me, but I had no idea of the depth of his love. To feel even a little of it is stunning.

I had no idea, Sherlock. I had no idea. I knew I was the "master," but I didn't have any grasp of the concept of being his alpha. Now I know what an honor it is to be an alpha. It is also a great responsibility. I must always live up to his expectations. I will try.

One thing I have picked up from him is his feeling that humans can be pretty dumb. I think he tries to conceal it from me, but he can't. And, my friend, he won't get any argument from me. I'm looking forward to years of getting to know him better.

It seems that I have inherited a pack. The Heinleiners have brought dogs along, and they are all CECs. What would be the point of a new world, a fresh start, if we didn't have dogs with us? I understand that Mr. Heinlein himself was a cat person. I can forgive him for that, and I've seen a few cats around. Sherlock gives them the stink eye, but he knows better than to make any trouble.

So . . . my pack?

The Dalmatian—who I now know is named Spike—was the alpha of his pack of free canines. When they had patched him up, he approached me cautiously, sniffed my hand, then rolled over on his back so I could scratch his belly. This meant he accepted me as the new alpha. A good thing, too. I'd have hated to have had to fight him for it. I saw how fierce he could be. How fierce all of them could be, working together. It is no mystery to me how wild wolves were able to bring down a caribou ten times their weight.

A bit of my hero status has rubbed off on the pack. People saw how they attacked the warrior, protecting me, and incidentally, Gretel. There is always a scoop of ice cream waiting for any of them at Hazel's new parlor, and so many handouts at the restaurants aboard that they are all in danger of getting fat.

———

What is an ex-peeper to do in this new world, on its way to another new world? Nobody deadheads on the *Heinlein*, believe me. I would cheerfully have worked in the warehouses, swept up the corridors, or gathered the garbage, but I didn't have to.

I wear two hats now. One is really just a continuation of my old hobby. I have registered Sherlock and myself as a

JOHN VARLEY

small business, the only private-detective agency within seventy billion miles. I don't figure we'll get much work, but then we never did. It's important to Sherlock, so I did it. We expect our first case any day now. If you need a dame tailed, just give us a jingle on the blower. We will shadow her to the ends of the ship. If you want any Maltese Falcons located, we're your guys. We are also available for recovering crown jewels, finding secret Nazi bases in space, and tracking giant hounds across the moors. As a sideline we do birthday celebrations, bachelor and hen parties, bat and bar mitzvahs.

My second hat is no surprise, either. I'm a cop again.

Heinleiners like to think of themselves as special in all ways. This is an exaggeration. They are special in *some* ways . . . but they are just like the rest of us in most ways. Some people steal. We need cops to catch them. Some won't wash. Can't have them stinking up the ship. We will be bringing felonies and misdemeanors and violations to Goldilocks along with all our virtues.

If anything, these people are maybe a little *more* prone to violent crime than your average citizen. Most of them are armed, for one thing. Some of them could do a lot better at impulse control. There have been, and there will be, arguments, and some will degenerate into violence. Fistfights the Heinlein Police Department will mostly tolerate. Gunfights, not so much. We have courts, and a jail. And there's always the air lock for extreme cases. Heinleiners do believe in capital punishment for the worst of the worst. I'm with them there.

One of the unwritten tenets of the Heinleiners is "An armed society is a polite society." This is bullshit. Maybe in ten thousand years, when all the hotheads and assholes have killed each other and brought up no offspring in their wild antisocialism, but I doubt it. "An armed society is a society where a lot of people are going to be killed by guns." It hasn't happened so far, but it will. It will.

One of the advantages of being a cop in the *Heinlein* is that there is nowhere to run, nowhere to hide. The ship is huge, but completely mapped, and covered by CCTV so complete you don't dare pick your nose. There are no hide-outs. Like a legendary police force from a frozen northern country back on Old Earth, the officers of the HPD are always going to get our man.

Oh, and Sherlock is an officer, too. Our department is small, only eleven people to run three shifts covering many thousands of passengers. Sherlock is the entire K-9 Division, though he has on call his Barker Street Irregulars if more dog-power is needed.

I don't have the faintest notion of how Mr. Smith's "hyper-drive" works. I doubt if more than three people do, and two of them might be faking it. Whatever it is, it gets us moving along quite smartly. At the midpoint of our trip, our speed will be frightening. I don't know how fast, and I don't really want to know. Apparently our clocks will slow down. I don't understand that any more than Sherlock would.

The hyperdrive doesn't seem to use much in the way of fuel. There are no big tanks anywhere on the ship, but it keeps thrusting away, twenty-four/seven. It also seems to involve some way of generating artificial gravity, as everyone is always well grounded. And though the ship was designed and built to provide spin "gravity," it doesn't spin. The view from the observation lounges is as steady as the stars seen from Luna. Steadier, as those stars also move as Luna rotates, just a wee bit too slowly to be seen.

We are now many billions of miles from the sun. All realistic previous proposals for starships have involved trips measured in centuries. Not this one. The trip will take about thirty-five years. I expect to be alive to see landfall.

The only painful thing is to realize that Sherlock probably won't. But even there, there is hope. I've spoken to some of the biologists aboard, and they are intrigued at the possibility of extending human life spans to dogs. There's no guarantee, but it could happen.

Meantime, I am going to enjoy the time I have with him.

In fact, I think I'll take him down to the nearest park right now and throw some balls for him.

(I promised Sherlock that he could have the last word.

(Yes, it is I, Penelope Cornflower, C.C.A.T., faithful transcriber. Though I never lived in Irontown, my mother was a Heinleiner and booked passage for me when I was very young. That was when getting the Heinlein *off the ground was a completely blue-sky idea,*

and one that most people thought would never happen. Sadly, my mother died in the Big Glitch.

(I have met Christopher Bach at last, and am now spending a lot of time with him, teaching him to communicate with Sherlock. He is coming along well though I don't expect him to ever equal my 97 percent adept rating.

(He is cute, in a rough-edged way. Strong arms, a manly chin, a tight little ass, always a plus in my eyes. I'll bet he could bench-press me all day long.

(Romance? Too early to tell, though I have insisted on taking him to one of the small beaches for whispering lessons, and have been sure to remove all my clothes and put my not-inconsiderable charms on display. No tugs on the line yet. I know that first I would have to lure him away from that Gretel, not an easy chore. I have to decide if he's worth the work.

(Of course he loves Sherlock, a factor which weighs heavily in his favor as a possible romantic partner. I don't think I could love a man who is not a dog person. I'll have to add up all the pluses and minuses soon.

(There is no hurry, though. The ship will be a long time getting to where it's going.

(Signing off for now. Over to you, Sherlock.)

—Penelope Cornflower
Certified CEC Adept (TEB 97%) Translator
Level 54, Deck G, Room 1101F
Robert A. Heinlein, *en route to Goldilocks*

epidog

Chris and I used to live in a place called Luna. Now we live in a place called *Heinlein*. One day we will live in a place called Goldilocks.

I do not understand all of this. This place called *Heinlein* passed places called Mars and Ceres and Jupiter and Neptune. We did not pass a place called Charon. I have learned that the place called Charon was far away, and is getting farther away all the time. I would have liked to have seen Mars and Ceres and Jupiter and Neptune. I would not have wished to see Charon. I bit a human from Charon, and I have learned that Charonese humans are very bad people. They would not be happy that I bit one of them. But I was happy that I did.

The Charonese person did not move after I let him go. I believe he was dead. I do not think I killed him. I think αChris's shooting him in the mouth probably killed him. But maybe I killed him. I do not care. He was a very bad person. αChris says I should not make a habit of biting bad people, though. I told him I would not.

I have a new job in this place called *Heinlein*. I am a police dog. I am called a K-9. I have always been a canine, but now I am a K-9, too. Ha-ha!

I like being a police dog. I have a badge.

This place called *Heinlein* is very much like the place called Luna only smaller, except that Luna was not going anywhere. Many things smell the same as Luna, but some things smell different. I am still sniffing out all the differences.

The parks are smaller. The plazas are smaller. Our apartment is smaller. I do not mind this, as long as αChris is there and there is plenty of food. There is ice cream in this place called *Heinlein*. How bad can it be?

I am very interested in this place called Goldilocks. I have learned that it will have very, very large parks. The parks in Goldilocks will be so big you cannot see the edges of them. This sounds to me like the parks I see in movies from the place called Old Earth. In these parks, I have seen dogs herding sheep. They were Shetland sheepdogs. I would like to do that. I have seen dogs chasing rabbits. I would like to chase a rabbit.

Miss Penelope Cornflower is here in *Heinlein*, too. She has met αChris, and they are spending time together. Miss Penelope Cornflower sometimes smells like she is interested in αChris. Human females do not have to be in heat to be interested. So far, αChris has not sniffed her butt.

(I only report what I hear from Sherlock, and am bound to do it faithfully and without blushing, if possible.—PC)

I have been thinking about many things. I have been thinking about this place called *Heinlein*, and how it is going somewhere. αChris took me to a place called the Observation Terrace. Outside the glass wall it is very dark, but there are many lights. The lights do not move. αChris says these lights are stars. αChris says that each of these stars is a place, and that there are other places around these stars. The stars look very small to be places, but αChris says they are very far away. Goldilocks is one of those places around a star. This is strange to me, but I still think about it.

Most of my pack is here in *Heinlein*. Two of them were killed in the big fight with the human from Charon. This made us all sad.

Lassie the collie had her litter soon after we came to *Heinlein*. There are one two three four five puppies. The humans said these were the first births in interstellar space. They are blind and can hardly move, but they know how to find the teat. They smell good. They smell like love. I have been thinking that I would like to make some puppies. I would love them and care for them. Wolf males help care for their puppies. I am mostly wolf, so that is how it would be. It would be good to run with them in the big parks in Goldilocks. We could chase rabbits together.

My nose has told me that somewhere in *Heinlein* there is a bitch in heat right now. She probably has most of the male dogs in *Heinlein* sniffing her butt and trying to mount her. But I am now a bold dog, and the canine leader of my pack. I think I may go find her and tell those other male dogs to back off because Sherlock is here.

Or I may just go to the park with αChris and chase balls.

JOHN VARLEY is the author of the Gaean Trilogy (*Titan*, *Wizard*, and *Demon*), *Steel Beach*, *The Golden Globe*, *Red Thunder*, *Red Lightning*, and *Rolling Thunder*. He has won both the Nebula and Hugo awards for his work. Visit his website at varley.net.

Ready to find
your next great read?

Let us help.

Visit prh.com/nextread

Penguin
Random
House